LYNTON
BUYS
A
NEW CELL-PHONE

AND HEARS
THE VOICE OF DOOM

by

J. Wayne Frye

A NOVELLA

Note to teachers: This book is written in Canadian English, so discrepancies in the spelling of words should be explained to students in other countries. In the vocabulary section, all words are spelled in Canadian English and the definitions are based upon the meaning within the context of this book. It is suggested that a review of the vocabulary precede the reading of each chapter.

ABOUT THE AUTHOR

Wayne Frye's *Aaron Adams* mysteries, *Chablis Louise Chavez* thrillers, *Girl* books and *Lynton* adventures titillate the brains of those who enjoy tantalizing tales. His life, like the heroes he writes about, has been filled with adventure and excitement.

He has been a college hockey coach, professor, and at one time, the youngest university president in the USA. Called a marketing genius by the *Los Angeles Times*, he has been a promotional consultant to hockey teams and motion picture companies. He has been cited for his work with inner-city gangs in Los Angeles and is active in the anti-globalization movement. A proud Canadian, he divides his time between Ladysmith, British Columbia; Laguna, Philippines and Cape Town, South Africa. He provides satirical political commentary to many Canadian newspapers.

Some of the 44 books by J. Wayne Frye

White Meteors and the Ghost of Sue Ann McGee
Hockey Mania and the Mystery of Nancy Running Elk
Something Evil in the Darkness at Hopkins House
How Hockey Saved a Jew From the Holocaust
The Girl Who Stirred up the Whirlwind
The Girl Who Motivated Murder Most Foul
The Girl Who Said Goodbye for the Last Time
Sammy Sasquatch and the Sts'ailes Star
Fall From Apocalypse
Armageddon Now
Worth Part 1: Roaring Through life Like a Comet in the Midnight Sky
Worth Part 2: The Night of Thunder Road
When Jesus Came to Jersey as the Son of Thunder
When Jesus Came to Canada to Lead an Indigenous Rebellion
Canadian Angels of Mercy – Nurses in Times of Peril
Points of Rebellion: Aboriginals Who Fought for Justice
Lynton Walks on Water
Lynton Curls Her Hair
Lynton and the Vampire at Tagaytay Manor
Lynton Buys a Cell-Phone and Hears the Voice of Doom
Lynton Viñas and Beowulf Perez in the Taal Inferno
Lynton and the Ghosts in the Mansion on Balete Drive
Lynton Viñas: Shadow in the Darkness
Lynton's South African Adventure
Lynton, the Karoo Vampire and the Jewels of Omar Bin Abi
Lynton and the Stellenbosch Terror
Chablis: Avenging Angel for the Forgotten
In the City of Lost Hope
Chablis and the Terrorist
Pursuit
The Disappearance

J. WAYNE FRYE

TABLE OF CONTENTS

LYNTON BUYS A NEW CELL-PHONE

TO:

<u>Channa Mendis</u>
Who shared an adventure with Lynton,
and is always there when needed.
She is a loyal, dedicated friend.

And of course, as always, to my beloved muse,
<u>Lynton Viñas,</u>
whose smile, infectious mannerisms and vamping
motivate, delight, titillate and mesmerize all who
gaze upon her outer beauty while delighting in
the inner beauty that radiates from the soul
of an extraordinary woman.

ISBN: 978-0-9879728-9-7

Fireside Books – Victoria, British Columbia/Port Angeles, Washington
Peninsula Publishing Consortium

J. WAYNE FRYE

PROLOGUE
JOURNEY INTO FEAR

For those readers who did not read *Lynton Curls Her Hair*, a review of that work is important before detailing her latest adventure. You see, Lynton is an extraordinary young woman who lives in a place called Cavite, which is about one hour south of the metropolis of Manila in the Philippines. She is in love with a man named Wayne who lives in Canada, and it is her fondest desire to be with him on an island where he lives in the Strait of Georgia near Vancouver, British Columbia. In the previous adventure, she was desperately wanting to get her hair digitally curled, but thought it an extravagance that simply made no sense. Her boyfriend, while visiting her, realized how much she desired this rather inexpensive procedure (about $80 Canadian), and he never revealed to her his plan to arrange for the procedure as a Valentine's Day present after he returned to Canada. It was that simple act which solidified Lynton's love for him, because it was so unexpected. It had nothing to do with the money spent, or even the nature of the present, because material things were of no importance to Lynton. It was the thoughtfulness and clandestine way her boyfriend, Wayne, conducted the whole affair. Now, one must understand the mystique and temperament of Lynton to realize that she is a woman with great depth of character, who describes herself as just a simple girl with simple tastes. She is well-known by all who encounter her as a woman of substance who refuses to bend against the winds of tyranny and never lets adversity get her down. Vanity is simply not within her nature. Although she had a new spring in her step and was more self-confident as a result of the new hairstyle, vanity simply wasn't within the realm of possibility for a woman who looked upon herself as just an ordinary woman who happened to be attractive. Although, she usually said that she was only attractive in her darling Wayne's eyes, because he saw her differently as a result of his deep, abiding love.

While Lynton was getting her hair done, in a small North Carolina town, another woman named Letty was also having her hair curled to give it more body, and make her, hopefully, in her mind at least, more appealing to men. Unfortunately, vanity made her entire personality change when she realized she had become a beautiful woman. In reality, this vanity made her beautiful on the outside, but ugly on the inside.

LYNTON BUYS A NEW CELL-PHONE

So, unlike Lynton who never was affected with vanity, this vanity actually destroyed Letty.

With this background information on Lynton's personality and demeanour, we now will explore how this extraordinary young woman, although non-materialistic, unwittingly used her feminine wiles to get her boyfriend to buy her a new cell phone. This act would lead her on an adventure with her friends Channa, Ingrid and her brother Robert that would raise the hair on the back of their necks and lead to what would be an exciting, spine-tingling journey into fear.

J. WAYNE FRYE

CHAPTER 1
SINISTER ELEMENTS AFOOT

Ingrid was Lynton's dear friend; she lived in a stately mansion in Laguna, Philippines which is in the metropolitan Manila area. Although the ornate home was an example of grandeur, it was not overly ostentatious, as Ingrid and her mother lived lives of relative frugality. They had a kind and gentle nature which endeared them to all. However, sometimes kindness can be mistaken for weakness, and Ingrid was certainly not weak.

LYNTON BUYS A NEW CELL-PHONE

Among the rich you rarely find a really generous person, even by accident. They may give their money away, but they will never give themselves away; they tend to be egotistical, secretive and self-indulgent. To be smart enough to get all that money they tend to be worshippers of self. However, Ingrid and her mother were the exception, not the norm. Theirs was a generous, kind nature to all around them. They embraced diversity and accepted people for the content of their character, not the size of their bank account.

Now, around their mansion, over the years, the area had become extremely blighted and the opulent neighbourhood had taken on a very distinct air of growing decay. However, these two fine people were gregariously accepting of their much less fortunate neighbours due to their kind, non-arrogant, magnanimous ways. However, there was one neighbour who lived directly across the street in a home that could only be described as foreboding.

LYNTON BUYS A NEW CELL-PHONE

The Evil House Across the Way

Across the street is a lonely house I know
That became evil many a summer ago,
And left no trace of love within its walls,
And there no daylight falls.
It is where evil incubates and grows.

Its shrubs from prying eyes are a shield.
Are there ghosts there afield;
The old man living there looks like a corpse,
And eerie sounds within abound.
There is an abiding evil to the sound.

I look at it with an aching heart.
I cannot from it feel far apart.
On that disused and forgotten path
There seems a beckoning call
That will make evil night fall.

The ravens flitter overhead and shout,
And a hush of death is all about.
I hear the devil from across the way

J. WAYNE FRYE   11

LYNTON BUYS A NEW CELL-PHONE

To have his evil say,
And take souls for pay.

It is under the small, dim star.
I know not what evils there are
Who share the unlit place within me,
Like stones under the low-limbed tree.
Oh, my soul, the evil there it does see.

That house is whining and sad.
It knows no modern fad.
From there no one ever sings
In the view of how many things.
It is as if the house had fangs.

Now, one might logically ask what does a house of apparent evil have to do with the purchase of a cell-phone. Be patient reader, be patient, because while Ingrid stood on her balcony gazing upon the ill-fated house of doom and feeling cold chills run up and down her spine, in Cavite, Lynton was talking to her dear Wayne and revealing to him something that would touch his heart and his pocketbook.

Skype phone calls on the internet were the bridge that kept these two lovers in constant contact. Wayne called it the life-line of love. As he sat in his office back in Canada, Lynton was about to weave a tale that would make Wayne recall something his father told him when he was a teenager – "Son, women don't come cheap."

Lynton and Wayne had been romantically involved for about six months, and during this time, Wayne had always been impressed with Lynton's refusal to ask him for anything. She felt that it was inappropriate to ever expect him to pay for anything she wanted. However, he had surprised her with a digital hair curl for Valentine's Day. On this particular day, Wayne was having trouble getting a clear picture of her on Skype. He kept telling her to adjust her camera, until she finally said, "Wayne, that is not it. You see, my brother needed a good cell phone for his new job, so I gave him my Samsung Galaxy, and I took his old piece of junk phone. I am sorry about the poor picture quality, but he just couldn't afford a new phone."

Wayne knew of the kindness that was inherently part of Lynton's personality, so he was not surprised at her magnanimous gesture. He asked her very politely, "So, you actually need a cell-phone then?"

"Yes, I am going to save for one. My dream phone is the Sony Xperia Z-1, but it is 24,000 pesos (about $600 Canadian dollars)."

Wayne, always a frugal man, who himself was one of the few people who did not own a cell-phone because of this frugality said, "That sounds awfully expensive. Wouldn't a cheaper phone or a used one be adequate to satisfy your needs? I mean 24,000 pesos, come-on."

LYNTON BUYS A NEW CELL-PHONE

"Yes, I suppose it is extravagant," replied Lynton in a soft, almost whispery voice.

"Lynton, why don't I send you some money for a used phone? I can afford it with no problem," Wayne offered enthusiastically, despite his misgivings.

Lynton was shocked that Wayne would offer to do that. "No, no Wayne. It is not your responsibility. I never want to accept any money from you. I am not your wife," and then an anticipatory tone crept into her voice, "not yet at least."

Wayne let a smile slowly creep across his face, because he knew it was Lynton's dream to be married, because she actually felt 29 was old. He laughed and said, "yeah, not yet, but I feel awfully hen-pecked, so it is only a matter of time. I am getting lots of practice in letting you run my life."

Lynton said, as she lowered her head slightly. "Well, I did not know I was hen-pecking you Mr. Frye." Then she performed that little movement of her head to the right, smiled just a bit, blinked her eyes and gave him that coy expression. Wayne called it vamping. Whatever it was, it had a profound affect on Wayne every time she did it, and it titillated his libido. He understood she knew what she was doing, but he found it cute and endearing. He let her control him, because he wanted her to do so. She knew that he got enjoyment out of it, too. However, she used it sparingly to make sure it never lost its effectiveness.

Now Lynton was not prone to extravagance, and she had been to the dentist recently and knew she had two cavities that needed filling. Normally, she would have been wise and have used her money for a visit to the dentist, but she had her heart set on the new Sony Xperia Z-1 cell-phone. It had become almost an obsession with her. She kept looking at other phones, but always kept coming back to the Sony.

It is not the purpose of the author to suggest ulterior motives, but Lynton knew Wayne, although not rich, was a man who had a pretty comfortable life, primarily because over the years he had managed his money so well. Whether it was conscious or subconscious, and maybe it was a bit of both, she wound up accepting Wayne's offer of paying for a used I-Phone. However, in the back of that pretty little head were visions of a Sony Xperia dancing about merrily like pixies in an open field.

Wayne checked several internet classified ad sites in the metro Manila area, and soon discovered that a new I-Phone 4-S was available for $400, so he decided to send her the money and said, "Pick it up at Western Union. Check out the I-Phones and see what you can get for that amount of money."

LYNTON BUYS A NEW CELL-PHONE

For several days Wayne kept looking for cell-phones in the 16,000 pesos ($400) range on various sites, but every time he and Lynton talked she kept discussing the Sony Xperia. As mentioned previously, it had become almost an obsession with her. In order to comprehend why, it might be advantageous to reflect a bit on Lynton's childhood.

The Philippines is a poor country that was first colonized by Spain, and then basically annexed by the USA as a result of the Spanish American War. Although called a democracy by the USA, the truth was compliant dictators were installed with American approval in order for the nation's natural resources to be exploited and for the USA to use it as a military base in its insane preoccupation with communism after World War II. So, young Lynton grew up as the apple of her poor farmer father's eye, but from a young age had to help put food on the family able. Therefore, she knew poverty's pinch.

J. WAYNE FRYE

LYNTON BUYS A NEW CELL-PHONE

However, by the age 16 she had moved to the city and was living in a house rent-free while attending school. She came home one day to see all her belongings out in the street. The house had been sold without her knowledge and she had nowhere to go. Thanks to the kindness of her friend Ingrid and Ingrid's mom, she would spend the next three years living with them. So, adversity had dogged her during the formative years of her life. Despite having to struggle, she endured with a cast-iron will that never let things get her down. Still, she lived a life on the fringes of survival in a nation like so many, where the economic structure benefited the wealthy at the expense of the poor. So, it is understandable that a luxury like an expensive cell phone was something that seemed to make her giddy with excitement. In a world where corporations propagandize people into believing the good life can only be enjoyed with material things, who can blame a girl from a poor background getting excited about a simple item like a cell-phone.

LYNTON BUYS A NEW CELL-PHONE

Perhaps Lynton was unaware of how Wayne lived for the privilege of seeing her happy, and did not realize that her constant talk of wanting an Xperia was tugging at his heart strings. He had never known want, because, although not excessively rich, his father was an entrepreneur whose success made him modestly well-off until, of course, Wayne's mother got sick. And in the USA, where healthcare is a privilege rather than a right, illness can wipe families out almost over night. This had happened to Wayne's father, and he saw years of hard work go for naught as medical bills piled up. Although his father recouped much of his losses, he was never the same after that. So, Wayne had a sense of what it was like to be poor, although he had never personally experienced it. He understood that a quality cell-phone was a luxury to Lynton, and that she longed for something that was frivolous. Of course, Wayne never got pleasure out of doing something for himself. It was doing for those he loved that brought him the greatest joy.

LYNTON BUYS A NEW CELL-PHONE

Wayne called her and said, "Lynton, go to Western Union again. There's an extra 10,000 pesos there ($250) and get the Xperia."

Lynton pleaded with him not to do it, but he replied, "It has already been sent. Pick it up. I e-mailed you the address where you can get the phone for 24000 pesos ($600) in Manila. Get Channa to go with you. I sent an extra 2000 pesos (around $50) for gas and take Channa and Ingrid out for dinner. Have fun."

Lynton was overwhelmed with joy. It was what she had wanted all along, but she felt a sense of shame, because she knew that her hinting had contributed to getting extra money out of a self-confessed tight-wad. Then she said, "My brother Robert is coming along too, because he knows about cell-phones since he works for a cell-phone company. Baby, thank you so much. I love you not because of the phone, but because you are so good to me."

LYNTON BUYS A NEW CELL-PHONE

Wayne, ever aware of the wiliness of women, willingly acquiesced, not because he felt manipulated, but because he had a sense of great joy in doing something that would make the woman he loved happy. He justified the purchase with thoughts of all the money he had saved over the years through frugal actions. Why had he saved the money? Because it made it possible to do things like this for someone he loved. Always lamenting the spending of money, this time there was no pensiveness over what he had done, because he knew the joy the cell-phone would bring to a girl who worked 72 hours a week, and was always denying herself to help her brothers and sisters who depended on her.

So the stage was set for Lynton, Channa and Robert to take the one hour trip to Manila, where they would buy the cell phone, but would also get much more than they bargained for when they arrived at Ingrid's home afterwards. They had no idea that there were sinister elements afoot.

CHAPTER 2
ENTITIES OF EVIL DWELL WITHIN

Channa picked up Robert and Lynton Saturday around noon. There was great revelry as they made their way to Manila. Channa was a very prim and proper young woman who had been a beauty queen at one time. There was something mysterious and alluring about her. Her face, somewhat luminous, had a shiny tone to it. Her eyes were a piercingly sharp shade of brown. Eyebrows were seductively arched over the curve of her brow before dispersing onto an enchanting face that was framed with wavy, ebony-coloured hair that was pulled back in a pony-tail. Plump, ripe lips had a flirtatious, inviting curl to them. And to add just the right touch of intellectual charm, she wore large framed glasses that seemed to intonate a woman of infinite wisdom. Put all this on a long, lithe, toned 5:8 frame and you had a woman of almost unearthly beauty.

On the other hand, Lynton was a tiny mite of a woman who stood only 5:2 but exuded self-confidence and boundless energy that made her appear ten feet tall. She was a human dynamo whose natural beauty was entirely different from Channa's. In a quiet, unassuming way she exuded a savoir-faire that was almost disarmingly seductive to all who encountered her. An unearthly chill would fall upon any room she entered. All voices hushed and movement paused, as if time itself did not dare continue its incessant journey in the presence of such a creature.

LYNTON BUYS A NEW CELL-PHONE

There was always stillness about those who gazed upon her. She walked so gracefully that she appeared to float through the air, gliding effortlessly like a gazelle on the open plains, seemingly unaware of the effect her presence had on those around her. Her perfect lips curved into a smile, and her porcelain white teeth glistened like polished pearls. Her bronzed cheeks looked as if they had been brushed with star dust by angels who had come down from heaven to anoint her a chosen one of the god of beauty. Her thick lips were parted wide, and her words seemed to float in the air as if each one was the soft sweet whisper of unbridled hope in a world filled with hopelessness. Oh, and those twinkling, alluring dark eyes seemed to be beacons that could guide a man to paradise in her arms. Her beauty was so natural, it was almost unnatural. She was poetry in motion, and her body looked as if it was sculpted by Michelangelo in homage to the gods of elegance. And despite all this, she was a humble, unassuming woman.

LYNTON BUYS A NEW CELL-PHONE

Now, no doubt, Robert, who was a young man of considerable good looks himself, must have felt honoured to be in the presence of these two beautiful women, even though one was his sister. Ah, but this story is not about beauty, it is about how a simple cell phone led three women into an adventurous rendezvous with horror, but first we must go to the mall with Lynton, Channa and Robert to see exactly how an instrument was placed in Lynton's hand which would lead to this adventure.

The mall was filled with those who scurry about in the belief that happiness can be bought in a world where corporations manipulate people with promises of euphoria based upon material possessions. These three were not the typical prisoners of corporate propaganda, but on this day, Lynton had fallen prey to psychological manipulations by these entities, as she was convinced that a Sony Xperia would somehow make her life better.

LYNTON BUYS A NEW CELL-PHONE

This book is not an indictment of Lynton's desire for a phone, because there was nothing inherently wrong with that. We all need an occasional bauble of fancy to brighten lives that are often filled with the drudgery of struggle to survive in a world where the many must toil in obscurity so the few can have lives of splendorous excess that is derived from the sweat of the working class who are the servants in the wheel of exploitation in the capitalist system that enslaves most of humanity. Wage slaves need to feel their labour is rewarding them with some of the things that will brighten an existence that is far too often nothing more than a struggle for survival in a world that seems to have no compassion for those at the bottom of the economic ladder.

As Lynton walked through the brightly lit mall, her thoughts were of Wayne, and the love he showed her. She had been searching all her life for a man like him, a man who was able to value and treasure her for more than her physical beauty. She had found a man who understood her, a man who appreciated the goodness in her, a man who saw the depth of character she possessed.

Channa and Robert looked at her simultaneously, observing her trance-like state. Then they gazed at one another and said in unison, "Thinking about Wayne aren't you?"

Lynton replied, "I am always thinking of Wayne. I am here in the mall to get an Xperia, because of Wayne's love. He spoils me, and I have to be careful not to take his love for granite." They passed Kentucky Fried Chicken and she continued as she pointed at the restaurant. "Come on in, this is Wayne's favourite place to eat, and he gave me some extra money to treat you guys. Let's have some of the Colonel's chicken on him. It will make him happy that I shared a meal with you two."

LYNTON BUYS A NEW CELL-PHONE

While they were eating, Wayne sat at his computer, composing a poem, as he often did when he did something out of the ordinary like sending Lynton money for a cell-phone. He thought it would be fun to send Channa and Lynton a silly rendition of their journey to purchase the phone.

On Saturday in the land of heat,
Lynton and Channa to Manila did go.
One beautiful, prim and proper.
The other one short, gregarious
and daintily scintillating.

The mall was their destination,
where like two bees
they buzzed and hummed.
Look out men, you might get stung.

They both had a gorgeous smile.
Channa bought clothes for style.
Robert reminded Lynton that Wayne

LYNTON BUYS A NEW CELL-PHONE

gave her money for a cell-phone,
and that they should buy it
before all the money is gone.

But Channa grabbed Lynton by the hand,
And said, "Let's spend
Wayne's money in happy land.

Shop, shop, shop, shop!
They shopped until they dropped.
Shop, shop, shop, shop!
They just couldn't stop.

Channa moved about with glee,
gyrating with precision in the mall
her shapely form for all to see.
Little did she know she was heading for a fall.

Her credit was at the top.
Her spending going up, up, up.
She paid with credit card or cash.
She was developing a spending rash.

J. WAYNE FRYE

LYNTON BUYS A NEW CELL-PHONE

She begged Lynton for more money to spend.
But Lynton had little of Wayne's money to lend.
Poor Channa's spending knew no end.
Over the edge she did descend.

Shop, shop, shop, shop!
Lynton shouts, "You have to stop."
Wayne will get mad
and we will wind up sad.

Shop, shop, shop, shop!
The girls knew they had to stop.
They both were sane now,
making a solemn vow.

They decided to hide out
At their dear friend Ingrid's
to be safe from Wayne's wrath.
It was their only path.

Shop, shop, shop, shop!
The girls are afraid Wayne will call a cop.

J. WAYNE FRYE 31

LYNTON BUYS A NEW CELL-PHONE

The two girls are calming down,
But they know Wayne will have a frown.

Shop, shop, shop, shop!
Their spending makes a dramatic drop.
The phone is bought and a call to Wayne is made.
"Darling, I love you, but now we are afraid."

Lynton proclaims, "We have spent all you got.
And my dear Wayne guess what?
I love the cell-phone a lot,
But now we want you to buy us a yacht!"

After eating, as the three approached the cell-phone shop, a feeling of dread seemed to come over Lynton. Walking through the doorway sent a chill through her body. Why she thought. Why am I feeling this way?

A tall, thin man of maybe 40 approached them. He was slightly deformed, with one shoulder higher than the other. Although he could hardly be termed aged, he had a well-worn wrinkled face. However, he had a look of calm intelligence, and his eyes were mesmerizing, almost hypnotic. They were dim and blurred, fogged over almost. With a somewhat sinister grin, he seemed to hone in on Lynton, ignoring Channa and Robert as if they were not there. "Oh, my dear, you are here for the cell-phone of your dreams. You are an Xperia girl if I ever saw one." He motioned for her to follow him to the service counter where there was an Xperia that had just been taken out of the box. There were several other sales people about, but none seemed to even be looking at Lynton and the man who was clad all in black. Even Channa and Robert began to mill about the store, leaving Lynton to talk with the salesman. There seemed to be a pall that fell all over the place, a hazy fog appeared to descend from the ceiling, and it was as if time was suddenly standing still and seemingly everyone was frozen in place, standing like mannequins. Only Lynton and the man seemed to be alive as a stillness engrossed everyone else. All the others there were just inanimate objects. The man's voice had a steady cadence that seemed to be lulling Lynton into a dreamlike state.

The man said, "Yes my dear, a pretty girl like you deserves a special phone. Yes, a special phone for a special girl. Believe me, this is that phone. It will open doors for you into a world you never dreamed possible. This Xperia is magical. There is one who awaits your help on the other side of reality. This phone will let you bridge the world of the real and the unreal, but be sure which world you are in, do not get trapped in the wrong one, because there are creatures there that want to steal your soul and imprison you in darkness. A great adventure waits. You are the chosen one who will free those who have been awaiting rescue for so long. The magic is in your hands, and it will manifest itself at the right time. You must use caution though, because there will be forces at work that will want to destroy you."

LYNTON BUYS A NEW CELL-PHONE

Suddenly, the fog was lifted and the people became animated again. It was as if the interlude of time freeze had never occurred. Lynton stood there with the cell phone and receipt for its purchase in her hand, not remembering purchasing it. The man was no longer there, seemingly vanishing into thin air. He was gone, but his words were still fresh in her mind: "This phone will let you bridge the world of the real and the unreal, but be sure which world you are in, do not get trapped in the wrong one, because there are creatures there who want to steal your soul and imprison you in darkness."

She looked at Robert and Channa, who acted as if nothing strange had occurred. Smiling, Robert said, "See, you didn't need me to advise you on the purchase. You handled it by yourself. Good choice girl, because the Xperia is the best."

Channa., looking at the still trance-like state Lynton was in said, "What is it girl?"

Lynton, with a puzzled look, replied, "Where did the man in black go? I was standing there talking to him."

Channa, perplexed, replied, as she pointed to the young clerk behind the counter "what old man? That is the clerk you were talking to. He sold you the phone girl. You look like you are in the Twilight Zone. Earth to Lynton – come in Lynton."

Lynton smiled and thought that she was so excited about getting the new phone that she simply must have been daydreaming. Yet, it seemed so real. Oh well, she would not talk about it, because Channa and Robert would think she was crazy.

She was so excited, she totally neglected to call Wayne and talk to him. In fact, it would be three days before she would call, and it would make Wayne fret about what was going on. It was not like Lynton to be neglectful of him, but strange forces were afoot. And fortunately for Robert, he was taking the bus back to Cavite, so he would miss what would turn out to be a journey into horror - a trip using the road map of despair that would ensnare the girls in a web of terror that waited to embrace them and pull them into the grasp of evil.

Lynton was about to learn that in the depth of a winter storm of despair, she would find that within her was an invincible summer. And that invincible summer would emerge from despair and misery into the abiding love of a man named Wayne. In his protecting, loving arms she would find a safe haven, a place of infinite promise and possibility, a place where dreams never died but were manifested in the bright sunshine of hope.

As they made their way to Ingrid's house in Laguna, the new cell phone rang. Surprised at the ring, Lynton looked over at Channa and said in a questioning tone, "I don't even have my number transferred yet. What is going on?"

Channa, very calmly replied, "Answer it girl"

Cautiously, almost as if she was expecting something to be wrong, Lynton moved the phone to her left ear. A voice, low and calm said, "He will need your help. Be not afraid, but be very cautious." Then the voice changed inflection and became more intense. "Do not expect evil to be tolerant. It is insidious. It smothers good. Look it in the face and never turn your back on it. It knows no honour." Then the phone went silent.

Perplexed, Lynton could only stare straight ahead in disbelief. Channa, used her favourite phrase. "Earth the Lynton. Come in Lynton."

Lynton related to her what she heard, and ever the practical woman, Channa said, "Prank girl, just a prank. That is all."

LYNTON BUYS A NEW CELL-PHONE

Lynton, began to punch in her old phone number as she said, "No, this voice was too sincere. It is no prank. There is something strange about this phone." She began to fondle it very tentatively. "It feels so warm. There seems to be almost a heart beat to it, like it was alive."

Channa, with that little tilt of the head, a rising of the eyebrows and the pursing of her lips, which was her trademark expression, offered words of frivolity, "stop fondling that phone like you do Wayne when you two are together."

Lynton laughed and said, "OK, Ms. Prim and Proper. Still, I say there is something strange about this phone."

Now Ingrid was a charming girl whose stately mansion seemed to offer a welcoming embrace to all who visited. As always, she was excited to see her two best friends. They cavorted and laughed together until Lynton whipped out her phone.

Ingrid looked at it and said, "My, that Wayne must have been set back a pretty peso or two for that little item."

Lynton was proud of the fact that Wayne loved her so much he wanted her to have the phone, but at the same time was having problems over Wayne spending a week and a half with his ex-wife. His ex-wife worked for a First Nations band and Wayne had been hired to work on a history of the band. He was staying at the same lodge where his ex-wife lived and this just was not to Lynton's liking. Although, she had given him permission to go, inside she was actually seething with jealousy. In fact, she was so angry she didn't even bother to call him after buying the phone.

This episode would eventually make Lynton and Wayne learn more about each other. It had led to consternation because of neglect, suspicions and uncertainty. Yet their relationship would become stronger in the end. Their troubles would start over Wayne's insecurities and lack of trust. He would accuse Lynton of deception, but any deception from her would not be about a lack of love. It would be about her need to deal with her own suspicions about Wayne. She had endured pain without telling him, because she wanted to be magnanimous and understanding, but how could anyone understand about Wayne spending a week with his ex-wife under the same roof. Then going to a hotel where they had rooms across the hall from one another. And she would even see her come into Wayne's room as if she belonged there. The whole time Lynton would be in pain, suffering with anxiety and fears that he might once again return to the familiar and discard the new. Her lack of communication with Wayne would make him agonize over what he might have done without realizing that his insensitivity was a major factor. She had never been unresponsive before. So, he, for the first time, would find reasons to doubt her over the appearing and disappearing contact telephone numbers on her on-line phone which obviously meant she was talking to other men. Why shouldn't she? Wayne had spent a week and a half with his ex-wife. Yet, they would talk their way through it, and Wayne would simply decide that there was no reason to continue to beat a dead horse. What had been done had been done. He would tell Lynton that it no longer mattered, because their love had pulled them through trying times.

Like the wind whistling incessantly through the dark nights of loneliness, time carries away the deeds of uncertainty and with those who love deeply, the uncertainty fades into a soft stream that meanders through valleys, hills and plains to flow into a lake of harmoniousness. The pain Wayne would feel over jealous uncertainty would be assuaged, not by any admission from Lynton, but by her pleading that she was a good girl who had done nothing wrong despite appearances. She was so kind, so gentle, so caring, so sincere that

LYNTON BUYS A NEW CELL-PHONE

Wayne's heart would melt with empathy for a woman who had endured poverty, pain and misery in her life, but only desired to find the right man to make her feel loved and wanted in a world which was often hostile to her. She had found that in Wayne. And in her, Wayne had found the woman who would lift him from despair and guide him into the paradise of her arms.

Of course, all that would be in the future, but for now, the three girls were about to face horror that they never imaged was lurking across the street from Ingrid's home.

After sharing cordial greetings with Ingrid, Lynton and Channa went into her home and onto the balcony that looked out on the old house across the street. It stood there like a broken tombstone in a cemetery at night, the moonlight glistening off the roof, the light forming an eerie glow that danced about the doorway.

Ingrid said, "I always get a feeling of dread when I look at that place. It seems especially evil tonight. I saw the old man who lives there just pacing up and down on the porch earlier, as if he was afraid to go into the house. He looked over this way, and I could see his eyes staring right at me. They seemed to be pleading with me, almost begging, but for what?"

Suddenly, Lynton's phone rang, startling the girls. Lynton said, "Hello." Her face turned pale and she began to breathe heavily. She said nothing, just stared over at the house.

Channa, using her customary refrain, said, "Earth to Lynton, come in Lynton."

Lynton, still staring at the house said, "A voice, a man's voice – a deep, foreboding voice said the house awaits you and your friends. You must face your fears. You must not waver before the demons of darkness. Go. Go."

LYNTON BUYS A NEW CELL-PHONE

Ingrid and Channa laughed. Shaking her head, Ingrid said, "Oh, now you are hearing strange voices on the phone, girl. Maybe it is Wayne playing games with you, because you haven't called him to say thanks. Girl, you are going over the deep end! I think all the excitement of buying the phone has short-circuited your brain."

Lynton, never one given to excessive levity, replied "Guys, I am serious. There was a strange voice, and it was not Wayne. There is something weird about this phone. And there is something equally weird about that house. I bought this phone from an old man in black, but Channa and Robert said I bought it from a young boy. It was as if while I talked to the old man, everyone in the place was frozen in time, only he and I seemed to be alive. He said it was a magical phone that would open up the gates to the real and unreal, and I was not to get the two confused. Then, suddenly I am standing there with the receipt and phone in my hand and the man is gone. I don't remember buying it. There are forces at work that I don't understand. I am telling you this phone – this phone is like possessed. Yeah, possessed I am telling you."

Again, the girls laughed, but the laughter died quickly as they heard low moans come from inside the house across the street. They were mournful cries. There was a tone of pleading to them, almost as if some entity within was begging for help, begging for release from some unimaginable evil.

So, it was now time for these three girls to embark on an adventure that would forever change the way they viewed life, the way they deduced the real from the unreal. They were about to lift the curtain that divided the possible from the impossible that blinds the mind, and look into the unknown. What lay before them will be laid out here in detail. The inner story must be uncovered personally, by each reader, according to ability and desire. And should any reader fail to see, as these girls saw, the shadowed picture and conception of that to which one may well give the accepted title of supernatural phenomena, all I can say is your mind is closed, because the events that occurred over the next days are catalogued verbatim as they happened. Nothing is coloured or shaded.

Now Ingrid's house is situated, as mentioned previously, in an area where it stands out as a symbol of moderate opulence among the normal and often sub-normal structures that represent the existence of those who must struggle to keep their heads above water in a country that, like the entire world, has a pronounced difference between the haves and have-nots as a result of an economic system that aggrandizes greed.

At the base of a low hill sits Ingrid's house, rising stately into the tree covered surroundings beside small squatters' homes. Far around there spreads a wasteland of bleak and somewhat dilapidated homes mixed among small but relatively new town homes and vacant lots. And, of course, sitting across the street in what seemed a perpetual fog was the old house where these three girls would face the entities of evil that dwelled within.

CHAPTER 3
SO MANY TIMES BEFORE

When the mind of good lies fallow,
the evil can incubate and grow.
Good people must stand like kings and queens
against the evil that spreads like the wind.
The waterfalls of good are clear, free and high
that flow gently through these three damsels.
They shake off the dust of evil and
they all glisten with a light that shines
like a beacon through the darkness.

LYNTON BUYS A NEW CELL-PHONE

It was early evening, and the air was dense with humidity. The girls cooked some rice and walked outside to sit in chairs in front of the sari-sari store (small convenience store) operated by Ingrid and her brother. As is often the case with young women, the girls discussed their love-interests. Now Lynton had been enamoured with Wayne for about six months, and Ingrid and Channa were happy that she had found someone with whom she seemed so happy. They had gotten the opportunity to know Wayne during his visit, and although they questioned the age difference between Lynton and Wayne, they knew that Lynton had been looking for that special man for so long that they dare not put a damper on her joy. She had been single for almost three years after a somewhat acrimonious break-up with her previous boyfriend. Her happiness actually made Ingrid and Channa joyous too, because these three were like sisters. They shared a camaraderie and affection for one another that was marked by extreme devotion.

LYNTON BUYS A NEW CELL-PHONE

For perhaps another hour they chatted quietly and comfortably. The stillness of the night was suddenly shattered with the ringing of Lynton's phone. Again, the foreboding voice, almost in a whisper, said, "Tarry not, you must face that which needs to be addressed. He who suffers awaits your humble lift up from his despair. Go forth and face your fears."

Lynton, placed the phone down on her lap and stared at the old house across the street. Ingrid and Channa sat bewildered. Not a word was uttered as a pall of dread seemed to descend upon Lynton. Finally, Channa broke the silence. "What is it girl? Come on. Don't tell me it is that strange caller again?"

Lynton, taking a deep breath, replied, "Yes, yes, it was." She slowly rose from her chair, not taking her eyes off the house across the street and continued with words that seemed to sear into the psyche of the girls, "we are going to that house."

Channa, ever practical said, "OK, we'll walk over to the house if you want. I am not afraid of an old house. It is the old lecher who lives there who frightens me, but with my two brave sisters by my side, I shall walk into the valley where the shadow of death may lie and I will fear no evil."

Ingrid interjected, "OK, that is all we need, a Bible quote to gird us against evil. Thanks a lot Reverend Channa."

As the two girls laughed, Lynton, very serious in demeanour, said "This is no laughing matter ladies. There is something sinister over there that waits in the darkness of that house that is not a home."

Down the sloping bank they made their way. They crossed the street and stood in front of the house among the gnarled trees and untrimmed shrubberies. The bushes were matted, and the trees overhung them, so that the place was disagreeably gloomy. It was a place that seemed to have no life. It seethed with a dismal and sombre ambiance. This was a place where one genuinely sensed evil dwelled. As they moved slowly forward, an impression of the silent loneliness and desertion of the place seemed to embrace them with a sadness that penetrated deep within, making them feel hollow inside, feel that this was a place of dread and foreboding that harboured unmitigated evil.

One could imagine things lurking among the tangled bushes; while, in the very air of the place, there seemed something uncanny. Through the still twilight air, a faint sound could be heard. It was neither moan nor cry, just a steady whining noise. All three girls had a look of puzzlement on their faces. "There's something very evil about this horrible place; I feel it in my bones," said the usually demonstratively brave Ingrid. And then she stared at Lynton as to ask why they were there. Still, she, along with Channa, moved gingerly forward behind the diminutive, but determined Lynton.

The girls got to the porch steps and stopped, staring at the old oak entry door that was worn from years of being pounded by the tropical rain. The porch was rotted and looked dangerous to walk on. Lynton looked to her right at an old swing that had obviously not been used in years. There was no wind. It was perfectly still and a deathly silence seemed to permeate all about them. Then, the swing swayed back and forth as if an invisible hand was moving it. Suddenly, a gasp of astonishment was forthcoming from Ingrid, who, bending down on one knee, was frantically scraping dirt away from just under the porch steps. It was a metal container buried in the earth. She worked feverishly in the now fading twilight of the day until she finally pulled it out and placed it on the steps. Lynton, breathing heavily, her phone in her hand, said, "What do you think is in it?"

LYNTON BUYS A NEW CELL-PHONE

Just then, the phone rang, shattering the deathly silence. All three girls jumped with surprise. Lynton reached up and wiped sweat from her upper lip as the phone continued to ring. Channa shouted, "Answer it girl. Answer the damn thing and shut it up, before the owner comes out here with an axe and chops us up."

Pushing the answer button, Lynton gradually put the phone to her right ear. She did not say hello. She just waited, because she knew what it was. There was no number on the call display, because it was not someone with a normal number. The words spilled out ever so slowly, but deliberately. "Read it so that you will know the story of this evil place. Digest every word and take heed. You three are the mighty swords of hope for a house where there is no hope."

Then the caller abruptly hung up, and Lynton related what the voice said. Ingrid, now getting a bit frustrated almost whispered, "Read what?"

Channa, the one who was most practical, prim and proper, very articulately said, "I would likely deduce that what is being indicated by that discombobulated voice on that infernal device you bought today is to read what's in the box obviously, Einstein."

Lynton and Ingrid looked at each other, then at the box. Scratching her head, Lynton said, "Open it Ingrid – go ahead."

Ingrid with some trepidation, shrugged her shoulders and said, "No thanks. I'm not opening that thing."

Small, demure little Lynton arched her shoulders back, threw out her chest and walked over to the box. She took a deep breath, snapped the box latch and slowly and meticulously raised the lid. She bit her lower lip and paused ever so slightly, but then very quickly flipped the lid all the way open. She stood and stared into the box.

LYNTON BUYS A NEW CELL-PHONE

Lynton brushed away some dirt that had gotten onto the old brown flayed pages of a small notepad about 13 centimetres by 20 centimetres (about 5 X 8 inches) and maybe 1 centimetre (less than 1/2 inch) thick. She held it in her right hand, and adjusted it so the setting evening sun's rays allowed her to see the words written on the cover. Then, there came a strange wailing noise out of the house. It appeared to float through the front yard; there was a rustle of stirring leaves, then silence and a cold chill penetrated each girl, sending shivers through their bodies like a torrent of cold water was being dowsed over them. They backed slowly away from the house, as if turning their backs on it might allow something to grab them from behind. They stopped by the entrance gate and stood for awhile in silence looking at each other. Lynton gazed down at the book, held it up where the girls could see what was written on the cover. The words were scribbled by hand, but they were very clear as the sunlight danced about the cover of the loosely bound pages.

LYNTON BUYS A NEW CELL-PHONE

Channa broke the silence. "I don't believe it. I tell you, this is some kind of trick. This whole thing is nothing but some elaborate ruse. Maybe Wayne is behind this whole thing."

Lynton very calmly said, "No, Wayne would not do this. He enjoys having fun, but not at the expense of causing someone consternation."

Ingrid interjected, "No, I agree, Wayne would not do this, and the notebook deserves scrutiny. Let's go back to my house and read what is in it. Those words on the cover are chilling."

Lynton again held the book up in the twilight and just stared at the words along with the other girls. It was almost as if they hoped the words would somehow mysteriously disappear if they were just patient. Lynton looked intently at those words, and they seemed to be seared into her brain, almost pulsating with terror – *An Account of Demons in the House on Girabaldi Road.*

LYNTON BUYS A NEW CELL-PHONE

The Girls Face the Horror

As they walked across the street, each of them had a horrible feeling that we were being watched by preying eyes. They reached the confines of Ingrid's home, but the chill of terror did not subside right away, as only after a few minutes sitting on the balcony were they able to shake off the haunting dread that had seemingly followed them across the street. Just as they felt somewhat comfortable, there seemed to come again from within that damnable house a sound of wailing, and Channa said, "It is the wind."

Neither Lynton nor Ingrid replied. They just sit silently as they realized there simply was no wind. It was an oppressively hot night with not even a hint of a breeze.

"Look," Channa decisively said, "I will not go back to that place. I am not falling for this demon mumbo-jumbo, but neither am I discounting that something sinister is at play there." She then stared over at the house and a shiver went through her body as she visibly shook. "There is something vile, unholy and diabolical about that place."

Lynton, a woman with a soft and tender heart, but not one to let her emotions get the best of her, very calmly said as she opened the notepad, "Let us see what is said within these few pages before we make any rash decisions." And, thus begins the tale of a house all assumed was filled with evil. The account that follows is just as Lynton read it to her friends. It was written in the first person by a man who was simply trying to record some extraordinary events that had trapped him in the grasp of damnable evil.

Welcome to Hell House

I am an old man. I live here in this ancient house, surrounded by huge, unkempt gardens.

LYNTON BUYS A NEW CELL-PHONE

The people around this neighbourhood, no doubt, think that I am mad. That is because I will have nothing to do with them. I live here alone with my wife, who has not ventured out of the house in 20 years. I only go out early mornings most of the time to avoid seeing anyone. We live off rice which is delivered once a month in a 20 kilo bag and the vegetables I grow in the small garden in back of the house, hidden from prying eyes by the tall shrubbery that surrounds the yard. I live in darkness like no one could imagine. It is a darkness of despair, fear and loneliness. Though my wife is with me, we just inhabit the same space. Long ago the evil came among us and we no longer live; we just exist.

I have decided to start a kind of diary; it may enable me to record some of the thoughts and feelings that I cannot express to anyone; but, beyond this, I am anxious to make some record of the strange things that I have heard and seen during many years of despair.

LYNTON BUYS A NEW CELL-PHONE

Before buying this home, we had heard of its reputation. No one was foolish enough to buy it for 33 years as it just set empty all that time, until a foolhardy man like me, who can't pass up a good deal and scoffs at the supernatural, comes along and the real estate agent cuts the price so much that I can't resist.

I tried for a few years to trace the owners in hopes they might enlighten me about the strange occurrences here, but it was to no avail. In fact, one man in the Hall of Records simply told me, "The devil built that place. You would be wise to leave."

I must have been here at least two years before I saw sufficient evidence that this house was possessed with evil of the vilest form. It is true that I had, on at least a dozen occasions, seen, vaguely, things that puzzled me, and, perhaps, had felt more than I had seen. Then, as time passed, I became aware of something unseen, yet unmistakably present, in the empty rooms and corridors. It is often the unseen which is scarier than that which manifests itself clearly. It was usually nothing but a feeling, but then there was also that chill I felt at certain times, a chill that penetrated to the very inner core of my being, a chill that nearly froze my heart.

The first concrete evidence I had that something was amiss, was one evening at midnight. I was sitting reading. Without warning, the lights dimmed, then began to flicker very slightly, giving the shadows that danced about the room a greater depth of blackness, and whenever the light would stop flickering, it appeared the room was bathed in a colour like luminous blood that had been splashed all about. I could see it running down the walls, flowing onto the floor and it seemed to be edging toward me. I heard a faint, frightened whimper, and something touched my shoulder from behind, but when I turned there was nothing there.

LYNTON BUYS A NEW CELL-PHONE

That was the first time I experienced real fear. I sat transfixed, my heart pounding frantically. I felt incredible fear; but could think of nothing better to do than wait. For perhaps a minute, I kept glancing about the room, nervously. I just sat watching for what seemed an eternity, but it was, no doubt, only a few minutes. I became conscious of a faint glow in the far corner of the room. Steadily it grew; filling the room with gleams of quivering green light, then it sank quickly, and changed to sombre crimson that instantly flooded the room. The intolerable glare caused my eyes acute pain, and I involuntarily closed them. It may have been a few seconds before I was able to open them. The first thing I noticed was that the light had decreased greatly, so that it no longer affected my eyes. Then, as it grew still duller, I was aware, all at once, that, instead of looking at the redness, I was staring right through it, and through the wall beyond. I was looking out on to a vast desert filled with gloomy twilight that glistened with evil. The immensity of this evil scarcely can be conceived. It seemed to broaden and spread out, so that my eyes failed to perceive any limitations to the terror and the evil manifestations that awaited me within this place of horror. I was simply overwhelmed with dread.

Suddenly, I became conscious that I was no longer in the chair. I was floating above it, and looking down at myself still sitting there. A cold blast of air with the stench of death in it struck me, and I was propelled into blackness and an intense cold engulfed me and I shivered furiously. I was no longer whole; it was as if I was nothing more than the dust of my soul. Atrocious darkness seemed to creep all about me, and I became filled with fear and despair. Within the darkness that surrounded me, the faint outline of blood began to appear. I was overwhelmed with an intense feeling of loneliness as the blood began to devour the darkness. As the blood devoured the darkness, the faint outline of a house was gradually materializing. It slowly became apparent, that it was my house which was materializing.

As I peered curiously at the house, which was now being consumed by the creeping blood, out of the corner of my right eye I saw a new terror. It was a hideous looking form that grew upon my sight. It had an enormous head with horns, gigantic ears, and seemed to be looking at the house that was being devoured by the blood as if delighted. Suddenly joining this hideous thing was a black entity that appeared transparent. It had six arms and in each hand it carried skulls that had these prophetic words across the brows: Destroyer of Souls.

Then, all at once, another hideous creature came into view as it walked about the house that was slowly being devoured by the blood. This creature looked like a beast with a human head, and it was trying to enter the house, trying to take it over with its evil.

LYNTON BUYS A NEW CELL-PHONE

To my surprise, in an instant, everything had vanished and I was in complete darkness except for a three beacons of light that broke through the blackness and the transparent figures of three of the loveliest women I had ever gazed upon could be slightly seen in each beacon of light. Their loveliness, their comeliness, their goodness, their kindness could be felt by the light that bathed me in its warmth. The brightness was aimed right at my eyes and there was a feeling of calmness and hope as these three visions of virtue, sanctity and piousness danced before my eyes. A soft, melodic voice whispered "Here are those who will free this house of its despair. They will bring light where there is only darkness. They will bring hope where there is only misery. The wait for these three may be long and arduous, but patience is a virtue that will be rewarded. One of them will be chosen to receive a sign in a most unusual way. She will hear my voice one day, and she and her fellow defenders of righteousness will answer the clarion call to rid this house of evil."

LYNTON BUYS A NEW CELL-PHONE

As Lynton read those words, all three girls looked at her Sony Xperia cell-phone that lay on the table beside her. The voice she had heard on it so many times was the same voice the old man had heard that day. All three girls instinctively knew it. Could it be true? Were Lynton, Ingrid and Channa the three beacons of light preordained to do battle with the forces of darkness that had held that old house and its inhabitant's captive for so many years? Were they destined to destroy the evil with their mighty swords of righteousness, or would the evil win again as it had so many times before?

CHAPTER 4
STAND AGAINST EVIL

Channa broke the silence as the girls sit bewildered about what their next step might be. "OK, I am game girls. Let's kick some demon butt. I am for going over there and talking to that old lecher who keeps checking out Ingrid. I don't believe in demons or ghosts, but I do believe in evil. There is something evil going on there – has been for years, and we are the three who seem to have in some way been elected to take it on."

LYNTON BUYS A NEW CELL-PHONE

Lynton leaned back in her chair and looked at the house across the street. She pointed at it and said, "I don't understand that house. I never have. For years I have been coming to see Ingrid, and that house just sits there, seeming to ooze with evil. Everyone looks at that old man as some kind of devil. What we just read suggests he is just a victim of circumstances who cannot escape the evil of that house. I think he needs help. I say we help him."

Ingrid jumped up and said, "Let's rock and roll girls!"

Ingrid had a large German Shepherd dog name Riley. He followed the girls across the street like a great protector with bold strides and a cock sure manner. This would be Riley's rude awakening, because what waited was more than anyone of the girls or Riley anticipated. They were about to take a walk into a private hell reserved for those who dared stand against the evil across the street.

LYNTON BUYS A NEW CELL-PHONE

As they arrived at the broken down old brown gate, Riley barked and bounded toward the back of the house where a sluggish stream meandered through the back yard. The girls all rushed after him. At the edge of the stream, Riley was steadfastly sniffing the ground. Ingrid kept calling him, but he just ignored her. Finally, the three girls stood by the stream, and they, too, smelled something strange, but they could not deduce what it was. They scoured the side of the stream looking for some indication of what was attracting Riley's attention. Suddenly, a gust of wind came along and a tall thin bush behind the girls fell over almost hitting them. Riley turned toward the fallen bush and gave out a deep growl; stopped and pricked up his ears. Then, a loud, half-human, squealing sound seemed to come up from the stream while behind the girls a loud moan could be heard. Riley was now highly agitated and barking. He suddenly jumped across the stream, going after something in a nearby clump of bushes.

LYNTON BUYS A NEW CELL-PHONE

The barking only continued for a short time until the girls ran to the clump of bushes as Riley suddenly began to screech and then there was silence except for Riley who was lying on the ground whining in pain, bleeding from a gapping wound in the side that had almost laid bare his ribs. He was in writhing pain, and Ingrid's eyes filled with tears. There was nothing they could do but kneel beside him and gently stroke his wrecked body. Whatever had done this to him was a creature of great viciousness.

Riley was taking deep breaths. The girls heard something behind them, turned and there stood the old man. For some reason, they were not afraid, because they saw tears in his eyes as he said, "I am so sorry Ingrid. I have watched you and Riley for years. He is a loyal companion. You girls should not be here. This is no place for fine young women like you."

Lynton said, "We are here to help you."

Surprised, the old man said, "What? Help me? Oh my, years ago I wrote of seeing three beautiful women in a beam of light during a flight of fancy caused by some entity in that abominable house where I reside. Could you be the women of whom I was foretold?"

Channa, smiling replied, "You bet your life we are them, and we are here to kick demon butt."

The girls followed the old man into the house where he carried Riley to patch him up. He introduced them to his wife, Celeste and told them to call him Richard. They shared tea with him and his wife, and all the years of the three thinking these two were somehow mad, flowed into a river of calmness as they realized how they had misjudged them. These were two kind, sensitive people.

Lynton, looking at the clock on a nearby wall, realized it was time to call Wayne. "Oh, no!"

LYNTON BUYS A NEW CELL-PHONE

Now Wayne had become so accustomed to talking to Lynton three times a day that he became alarmed when he did not hear from her at the normal times. Being a beautiful young woman, who often had to be out late at night because of her work, was cause for concern to Wayne. So, Lynton realized he would be worried, but what happened next would make her forget about calling Wayne.

The living room was in the back of the house overlooking the stream where all the commotion had occurred. Suddenly a loud boom was heard and a stream of water seemed to be hurled upwards from the babbling brook. Celeste jumped to her feet and shouted "They are coming."

Telling her to stay where she was, Richard snatched up a nearby axe from the back porch, and ran toward the stream. The girls stood up bewildered and watched. As Richard neared the stream, there was dull, rumbling sound that grew quickly into a roar and up from the stream a fresh volume of water squirted into the air.

"I don't know why he is always taking that axe with him," said Celeste rather forlornly. "Like it will do any good against those demons."

Lynton asked, "What is out there. What is underneath that stream?"

Celeste very calmly said, "watch, and you will see that an abomination from hell is beneath the stream. Just watch. The thing in the bottom of the stream will slowly appear. It has been trying to get into the house for years. Only my dear husband has kept it at bay all this time."

The girls were transfixed on the back yard and the old man. They saw a vapour began to rise from the creek bed. There was something below to the left of the old man that began to take form. They all looked intently toward it and made out another, and then another shape. Three dim shapes that appeared to be climbing up the side of the steam. They could see them only indistinctly. The shape in the middle began to take on form. It was a horrible creature with horns on its elongated head and nostrils that breathed fire. It had a hideously grotesque, gnarled face that had puss streaming out of giant boils.

As the thing glanced past Richard at the girls, it sent a cold shiver through them. There was a menacing countenance to the gaze. It gave a sudden, uncouth squeal, and the two other entities began to take shape. Richard swung the axe at it and it disappeared but immediately formed again. Richard turned and ran to the house. Then, the hideous entity hovered at the back door as he ran in. The door was locked, but it was banging on it and a low gravely voice said, "These three will not save this house or you. The years of keeping us at bay are about to end. This is the devil's playground, be gone. Be gone!"

LYNTON BUYS A NEW CELL-PHONE

Richard shouted to the girls and his wife. "The windows, close them and bolt them. They are so restless tonight I fear them as never before."

Just as the house was secured, sounds of whispering outside could be heard. Evidently, the hideous, malevolent creatures were feeling with their hands to see if there was a way in. They were making scratching noise with what seemed like claws.

"Why could demons not just go through the walls," shouted Lynton.

Richard pointed toward a series of plants hanging over the windows and doors. "Even a creature of the night, be it from hell itself, may be warded off with wolf-bane. It is not just to ward off vampires. Its powers are so mystical that even the devil fears it. That is how I have kept the creatures at bay all these years, but my garden grows ever scarcer of it, and this is not a country where it grows well. There are times when I do not have enough and the creatures have almost penetrated the walls."

Lynton remembered something she had once read and she repeated it for all to hear. "Eye of newt, and toe of frog, wool of bat, and tongue of dog, adder's fork, and blind-worm's sting, lizard's leg, and owlet's wing, for a charm of powerful trouble, like a hell-broth boil and bubble. Wolf-bane need not ward off only the blood-suckers but the demons of hell as well."

Ingrid, with a quizzical look said, "I assume you mean that wolf-bane keeps the demons at bay?"

"I do," replied Lynton as she seemed to exhibit an air of authority and knowledge. "I have read accounts of werewolves being warded off by wolf-bane, and I discounted them as ridiculous fanciful tales, but after tonight I am not so sure."

LYNTON BUYS A NEW CELL-PHONE

Channa chimed in her direct and forceful manner, "Yeah, I would say our concept of reality has been sorely tested tonight. What I believe has been altered appreciably here in this house. I am almost ready to believe in Santa Claus and the Tooth Fairy."

A deep darkness fell upon the house and there seemed to be weeping emanating from the walls as various cries and groans bounced about the rooms and corridors. It appeared that each crack and creak was alive with some ghastly thing that was trapped in that house. Yet, an even greater evil waited outside and wanted in to wreck further havoc in the place of evil.

Leave it to the diminutive Lynton to lead the army of girls and one brave man against the demons that were dancing a cavalcade of mischief. With great determination, as all the lights dimmed to leave the rooms almost in total darkness, she shouted, "Get us a flashlight, now."

LYNTON BUYS A NEW CELL-PHONE

As Richard ran to get a flashlight from the kitchen, Ingrid said, "What are you up to Ms. Ghostbuster?"

Lynton, never one to cower in fear at anything, said, "The voice on the phone said we are to go forth and battle evil. OK, let's see exactly what we are dealing with. No dead thing is going to scare me off. I am more afraid of the living than the dead."

As Richard entered, flashlight in hand, Channa nodded her head in the affirmative and said, "The boundaries which divide life from death are at best shadowy and vague. Who shall say where the one ends and where the other begins? We are about to find out the answer to that question. Let's take on these entities, whatever they are."

Ingrid, never one who was given to philosphical proclamations, interjected, "Fear not death. Fear an inadequate life. Let's get busy living, girls."

LYNTON BUYS A NEW CELL-PHONE

What can one adequately say about three women as exceptional as Lynton, Channa and Ingrid? Wayne had met Ingrid and Channa the second night he was with Lynton, because, for Lynton, it was important to get their approval of Wayne. You see, these three girls had forged a friendship that had been tested time and time again, and always they came through adversity more devoted to one another than ever before. It is only the great hearted who can be true friends. The mean and cowardly can never know what true friendship means, because they are unwilling to take risks with another person. True friendship can afford true knowledge. It knows neither darkness nor ignorance. These girls allowed no darkness to cloud their devotion to each other.

Wayne had been so taken with the friendship of these three beautiful women that he once told Ingrid, "Hey, when I fell in love with Lynton, I got a package deal. You and Channa will always be a part of our lives."

LYNTON BUYS A NEW CELL-PHONE

So, now these three determined women were about to go into battle against the forces of darkness. Their purpose had been fixed by a voice on Lynton's new cell phone, and they were prepared to set sail into a stormy sea of evil. The three of them stood together defiantly prepared to do their utmost or perish in the attempt, as they knew that they were in the eye of a storm of cataclysmic proportions. Yet, danger to these girls gleamed like eager sunshine in their eyes.

These three knew that courage was not the absence of fear, but the triumph over it. They knew the brave person was not one who denied fear, but one who conquers it. These women were strong enough to know their weaknesses, but brave enough to know that it is vain for the coward to flee, as death will come to all, but it is how you meet that death which defines you as a person. They were afraid yes, but they would not allow fear to keep them from doing what was just and fair.

J. WAYNE FRYE

LYNTON BUYS A NEW CELL-PHONE

Along with Richard, the three girls went from room to room, along corridors, and into the many little hidden nooks that formed the old house. Then, when they had surveyed every nook and cranny, they stood at the top of the stairs, but wailing noises continued unabated.

The four of them moved to the base of the stairs, and suddenly, they heard a crashing sound from the kitchen. They all hurried to get there but saw it was empty. Then, as they turned to leave, Lynton noticed two bright spots seemingly in the window by the back porch. She just stood staring. The others did an about face and stood by her side. The lights began revolving slowly, and throwing out alternate scintillations of green and red. They all looked at one another, as they knew what it was. The two lights were eyes.

The thing was moving and it appeared to be climbing. Lynton moved to the window. She realized that the creature's eyes were looking into hers with a steady, overpowering, compelling stare.

Channa shouted, "Lynton, what are you doing?"

Lynton, not taking her eyes off the thing gazing at her, replied "I am showing this abomination from hell that I am not scared of it. We came over here to fight evil, not to give into it, not to run from it, not hide from it."

Ingrid, frightened, but her courage bolstered by Lynton's fearlessness, determinedly interjected with supreme confidence as she glanced over at Channa, "Hey, you said we were here to kick demon butt. Let's do it girl." Then she turned her head toward Lynton and continued, "How do we fight these things, whatever they are?"

Lynton, turning her back to that evil entity, directed a question at Richard, "So, this is the nightly procedure of these things?"

Without hesitation, Richard replied, "It is. We go through something like this every night. All is quiet until twilight. We sleep days, because our slumber cannot withstand these evil entities bombarding us, trying to enter this wicked house."

Lynton, now growing in confidence, actually let a smile creep across her thick, luscious lips. "No, this house is not evil, and the moans, sighs and cries you hear in it are not evil either. Those are the screams, the pleadings of souls hiding here, hiding from these abominations from hell that want those poor tortured souls to come with them to the pit of fire that awaits those who have done ill deeds in their lives. People, I believe in neither heaven nor hell, but I believe in evil, and there is an evil that wants those trapped in the walls of this house, entities of those long dead who are hiding here to keep from being dragged into the fiery pits of eternal damnation. Those creatures outside want souls, souls that are hiding here."

LYNTON BUYS A NEW CELL-PHONE

Astounded, the girls, Richard and his wife, who had joined them, all had looks of disbelief as they stared at Lynton. Yes, Lynton had in one night figured out that which had perplexed Richard and Celeste for so long. Those entities in the house were not to be feared, but to be pitied.

Silently, they all stood in awe of Lynton's perceptiveness. Then, the silence was shattered. Suddenly, there sounded a quick low grunt, and the back door creaked under a tremendous pressure. It would have burst inward, but for the supports Richard had previously screwed into it.

One of the things squealed menacingly. Again the door creaked under a huge force and a pounding began. As it had for years, the braces held, and then followed horrible, grunting, muffled talk. They became quiet and as the dawn of day began to slowly arrest the darkness, those horrible entities seemed to hurriedly scramble back to the pit of hell from which they came.

LYNTON BUYS A NEW CELL-PHONE

There was an eerie quiet to the house as the sunlight began to peek through the windows. Like a symbol clanging in a church, like a bomb blast in the quiet desert morning, like a drum pounding out a fanfare that infernal cell-phone rang. Yet, this time Lynton reached into her pants' pocket for it without any trepidation or hesitation. What she first interpreted as the voice of doom, was not sinister at all. Yes, it foretold of the possibility of doom, but it was not the voice of evil. She answered without even saying hello. "Yes, what do you desire of me?"

The voice, now seeming more staid, less menacing and respectful, replied, "I had waited for so long. I saw person after person come into that store, but they were not right for the job that needed to be done. You had a bright light that surrounded you. There was a glow to you that sparkled with kindness, sanctification, purity and love. In you, I finally found one who is untainted by selfishness, self-interest and greed."

Lynton, never one given to self-aggrandizement or willingly accepting of any praise whatsoever, interrupted, "Listen, I don't need platitudes. I need specifics on what I am supposed to do here. I am just an ordinary girl with ordinary skills, and I believe neither in heaven or hell. All I believe in is what I can see and feel, and what I see here is definitely unexplainable, but it is, without question, evil. Evil I do believe in. I see it day in and day out. Why me? Why Channa? Why Ingrid?"

Very calmly the voice replied, "It is only by accident that you were friends with someone who lived across the street from the purgatory house. You were chosen because of the inherent goodness which dwells within you. That is no guarantee you can defeat the evil, but the two poor souls who have lived in that house have kept the demons at bay for nigh onto twenty years. They need relief from their burden. The souls have been trapped there far longer, but they need to be freed to go to another plain where their torment will end. Their recompense for sins is at an end, but as long as that gate to hell remains open for the demons to frolic about they cannot escape. They cannot free themselves. Their torment is excruciating. You and your friends have the power to end their agony."

Lynton, had turned her speaker on, so they could all hear. "So, you are telling me that this house is purgatory for souls who are between heaven and hell."

The voice replied, "Call it what you will. You are a non-believer, so you cannot accept that there is a heaven or hell, but believe me, there is evil. You have seen it firsthand, now. This evil will not stop until it has those souls that reside within that house. Beneath that stream lies a dominion where vile, insidious evil rules supreme. You three girls are pure at heart, as are Celeste and Robert. Goodness can defeat evil."

Channa, shaking her head, interjected, "Yeah good can win, but so can evil. In fact, based upon what I see in the world, evil generally comes out on top about 99% of the time."

Filled with deep emotion, the voice replied, "The world is a dangerous place to live; not because of the people who are evil, but because of the people who don't do anything about that evil." The phone then went dead.

Bowing her head as if mildly shamed, Channa had no reply to what the voice had uttered. Ingrid took a deep breath and sighed. Lynton bit her lower lip as in deep thought, then she looked at the other girls, took a deep breath and all three of them had a look of determination on their faces as they knew what they must do. They were strong. They were invincible. They were determined. They were forceful. They were undeterred in their mission. They were the mighty swords of hope that would slay evil.

CHAPTER 5
HOPE FOR THE FORGOTTEN

We make or break ourselves with life's choices. A fork in the road where we choose whether to go right or left has a profound effect on our future. It can be the difference between the dark and the light. Lynton was a young woman who was filled with compassion, but that compassion did not come at the cost of cold, logical reasoning that allowed her to assess a situation thoroughly before proceeding.

LYNTON BUYS A NEW CELL-PHONE

This was one of those situations. She explained to the four people there with her that undoubtedly the house stood between two worlds. It was a way-station for those souls who were doing penance for misdeeds, paying for their sins by suffering there. However, they had been ready for ascendancy to the plain of hope, as their penance had been paid, but the base of evil that surrounded that house would not let them escape. The evil entities wanted those souls. In fact, that was their stock and trade. The entities of evil were stealers of souls trapped in purgatory, and the house was a refuge where they pined to ascend onto a higher plain. Richard and his wife had unknowingly been vanguards defending the poor trapped souls.

As usual, Channa, in her articulate manner, said, "So, what is the plan General Lynton? We take them on face to face, or do we use subterfuge to fool them and catch them off guard. What's the deal, girl?"

LYNTON BUYS A NEW CELL-PHONE

Lynton turned to Richard and asked, "There are never any attacks during the day? Am I right, Richard?"

Richard nodded his head in the affirmative, and Lynton continued. "OK, so we are safe during the day. We can open the doors and windows without fear. We can go about our business as usual. These creatures only come out at night for some reason. Then the question is why can't these souls escape in the daylight?" Again she looked at Richard, "I assume that there are no manifestations of moaning, groaning and crying during the day?"

Again, Richard nodded affirmatively as Lynton continued, "So, they are trapped during the daylight hours, too. OK, we three have jobs to do before night falls. Richard, Celeste, do not fret, the three damsels of distress relief will be back before dark. We will take on these evil entities and like a mighty typhoon blowing through the island we will mow down distress, hopelessness, fear and despair."

There are those who think the devil is on God's payroll to meat out punishment as superintendent of hell to those who have sinned in life. It is not our intention here to debate religion, but it is germane to simply say that all three girls believed in evil, because they had seen it first hand the previous night.

Does God really keep the devil on his payroll? Is the devil the chief superintendent of hell measuring out punishment to the lost? Nearly the entire world is steeped in beliefs that there is actually a prince of darkness supervising a pack of demons deep within the fiery bowels of the earth with pitchforks jabbing sinners in the butt. Although this might seem unfathomable to enlightened, educated people, it is a belief used to keep people in line so they will fear retribution and therefore walk the straight and narrow path.

LYNTON BUYS A NEW CELL-PHONE

Lynton and her two friends had scoffed at a belief in hell. They still weren't convinced, but there was definitely something unexplainable afoot in that place of evil across the street from Ingrid's house. So, they were willing to accept the fact that there was unexplainable evil causing havoc, and that it was their duty to fight it.

Ingrid and Channa followed Lynton across the street. There was an assured cadence to Lynton's gait. She had grown steadily in confidence since meeting Wayne, because Wayne never stopped praising her for her intelligence, determination, kindness and beauty. She had called herself a shy girl, but now she was more self-confident, and she had a supreme belief in her ability to overcome any adversity. Channa and Ingrid had watched her with deep interest, because their love for her was unquestionable, unwavering, unshakable and enduring. They were proud to be her friend, proud to know that she was as loyal to them as they were to her.

LYNTON BUYS A NEW CELL-PHONE

They went up to the balcony; all took seats as Lynton placed the cell-phone on the table, pointed at it and said, "I urged Wayne to buy that phone for me. I wanted it so badly. You know what? He didn't think I needed it, because he is a frugal man who keeps an iron fisted grip on his money to make sure it is only used when absolutely necessary. Yet, he loved me so much that he could not deny it to me. I must be respectful of him, because his love is so profound that I could easily abuse it, but I will not ever do that. To him, thrift is not an affair of the pocket, but an affair of character. He believes someone who does not economize will eventually have to agonize. He has taught me that frugality can make you rich, and those who learn to practice it will avoid abject poverty. He says that it is disrespectful and uncaring for anyone to spend lavishly when so many go to bed hungry at night. Yet, I look forward to the day when I can tell him that this one act of lavish wastefulness on my part freed those who suffer anguish."

LYNTON BUYS A NEW CELL-PHONE

Channa said, "Yes, we all know Wayne's penchant for frugality. However, what does that have to do with what we must face tonight?"

Lynton, smiling broadly, replied, "It has everything to do with it. Don't you see? It does not matter what cell phone I bought. I could have purchased the cheapest model available, and I would have still heard the voice. I am so happy with my phone, but it is not the phone that really makes me happy. I realize that now. It is the love of the man who bought it for me. Those two people across the street in that abominable place that is surrounded by the demons of darkness are filled with love, too. All these years they could have packed up and left, but there was something that kept them there. They didn't know it, but they took on the job of protecting those poor souls that are lost within those walls from the demons of darkness that want to claim them. Wayne wants to protect me. He wants to show me a path to a richer and fuller life where love can be more than words. It can be deeds, simple little deeds that might seem inconsequential, but are at the core of what really matters in life. You cannot dismiss love from any equation. We three have such devotion and love for one another that we were chosen by that voice, by that thing, by some loving entity, whatever it is, that speaks to me on that phone, to save those souls from damnation and to free those two wonderful people over there from the anguish they have suffered for so long."

From a perplexed Channa came the question, "But what can we do, Lynton? How do you defeat the supernatural? How do we battle against demons that, until yesterday, I did not believe existed. In fact, I saw them. I heard them. I nearly felt them. Yet, I am expecting to wakeup from a nightmare any minute now. This is unreal to me."

Lynton looked at Channa, then Ingrid. She slowly pivoted her head toward the cell-phone on the table and stared at it intently. "We wait."

LYNTON BUYS A NEW CELL-PHONE

Ingrid said, "Wait for that voice again? Where is it coming from? I thought it was Wayne at first, just playing with you, but now I know it isn't Wayne. But what is it going to tell us, Lynton? What? I am bewildered and confused. I am afraid, too. So afraid."

"No, it is definitely not Wayne. He would never do something like this. I have learned more and more about him with each passing day. The one thing I know above all else. The one thing I never question. The one thing that he shows me each and every day is that he loves me like I never dreamed it possible to be loved. The voice on the phone is about love too. I thought it was the voice of doom at first, but then I realized that it was a voice of hope, reason and concern. That voice comes from another dimension, a place we cannot comprehend, a place where love abounds and where hope itself is a species of happiness, and, perhaps like all other pleasures immoderately enjoyed, hope in this case exists for those in pain across the street. Those souls await release from pain, and for some reason, we are the ones who can give it to them. That cell-phone was given to me out of deep, abiding love by a man who knew I did not need it, but who gave in to me for no other reason than love. He put aside his intense frugality, because his pleasure is derived from seeing me happy. My happiness is his happiness. That is why the voice used that phone. Don't you see? That phone is love. The kind of love Wayne showed me made it a conduit of that love. I walked into that cell phone store and that man or being or whatever it was had been waiting for the right person to come in fortified with love. He needed the right person to use in order to free those souls over there. I was that person, because I walked into that shop carrying love from a man who adores me. Time came to a standstill then and there. Time was frozen and stilled so that he could sell me this phone. The phone is not magical. It is the love that is the magic. That voice is love."

LYNTON BUYS A NEW CELL-PHONE

Channa, calculatingly perceptive and precise in everything she did, smiled and said, "Girl, you hit the nail on the head with precision. Love, yes, it is love."

Ingrid, somewhat perplexed, asked, "You are telling me that phone is love. That voice is love. OK, but how is that going to defeat those demons from the fiery pits of hell?"

Lynton took her gaze from the phone and said, "We don't need the voice any longer. The voice wanted us to help those souls and those two wonderful people over there who have been misjudged by all for so many years. Don't you see we are giving them hope with our love? Wayne's love for me and my love for him, and Ingrid and Channa, the love the three of us share with one another - that is what will defeat those demons. What I thought was the voice of doom is actually the voice of love, and that love offers hope for the forgotten, the weary, the desperate."

LYNTON BUYS A NEW CELL-PHONE

Hope is the thing with feathers
That perches in the soul
And sings the tune without the words
And never stops at all.

And sweetest in the gale is heard;
And sore must be the storm
That could abash the little bird
That keeps so many warm.

I've heard it in the chilliest land
And on the strangest sea,
Yet, never in extremity,
It asked a crumb of me.

J. WAYNE FRYE

CHAPTER 6

NOT FEAR THE BEAST

Unarmed truth and unconditional love
Are mighty, formidable weapons
In the battle of good versus evil.
Only an individual who knows
What it is like to be defeated
Can reach deep within the soul
To find that extra spark of hope
And the courage to go
Toe-to-toe with evil and not flinch.

J. WAYNE FRYE 103

LYNTON BUYS A NEW CELL-PHONE

Lynton was not one given to hyperbole, so she was very calm and precise with what she said to the two girls. "We are all sceptics when it comes to religion, because we have seen its intolerance. So, I shall not brandish Bible verses or invoke God, but I think we all believe in evil, because we see it every day in a country where poverty abounds in the midst of plenty, where corruption is the norm rather than the exception, where greed is allowed to debase human-beings so that profits become more important than people. I have been transformed by" and then she pointed at the cell-phone, "that instrument which lies there before us. I wanted it for all the wrong reasons, but through it I now know the true meaning of the love Wayne has for me. I also understand that if good people see evil they must stand against it. That house over there is not evil in and of itself. The people who live there we thought were evil incarnate are actually guardians against evil. Judge not until you have walked a kilometre in someone's else's shoes."

Channa interjected, "Yes, we have all learned something from that simple purchase of a cell phone. We are all more cognizant that the unreal is sometimes just as apparent as the real. All you have to do is open your mind to possibilities that you believed were impossible. I will not believe in fairy tales until I see Mother Goose in person or observe Tinkerbelle dancing on my bed. Do not tell me something is a miracle, because it was recorded as such by some individual. Show me proof. Show me cold hard concrete facts. I know what we saw over there, and that is fact in all our minds, so it is either a mass hallucination or it is real. I vote for real. I don't need an explanation. All I need is a way to confront those things, and I am one woman who will take my glasses off, ball up my fists and kick demon butt."

Ingrid laughed and said, "Channa, you are obsessed with kicking demon butt. OK, I am in girls. I don't know how we are going to do it, but it will be dark soon, so let's make plans."

LYNTON BUYS A NEW CELL-PHONE

Lynton offered some sage advice. "Wayne has taught me one very important thing. You must arm yourself with knowledge before doing anything. Before he let me get that Xperia, he researched, pondered and reviewed almost every make of cell phone. Of course, there were cheaper ones just as good, but he knew I wanted this one, so he acquiesced to my manipulations and just laughed at how I vamped him. Lucky me, he thought my manipulative vamping was cute. OK, well he made sure that he, me and Robert were all equipped with knowledge before going to get it, and we need to equip ourselves with knowledge before battling those three demons."

"And how do we do that?" asked Channa.

Lynton turned toward Ingrid and said, "We get on Ingrid's computer and look up *experts on demons*, and find a knowledgeable person who can give us some advice. If there is no person in the Philippines who can help, we will at least find information on the history of demons. We know what they look like. There may be pictures with explanations."

The girls scoured the internet for information. There was a professor at De La Salle University who specialized in demonology. They called and made an appointment. On the way there, Lynton thought, "Wayne would be proud of me."

Professor Renaldo Hernandez was a short, rotund Filipino with a mop of white hair that seemed to have fought a battle with a typhoon and lost. His eyebrows were thick and arched upward in the middle, making them seem like horns. His eyes were constantly blinking and he had nervous tick that made the right side of his mouth twitch every few seconds. He was obviously enthralled by the story told by the girls, but in the end simply said, "Demons are a fact. I have never personally seen one, but I believe they exist. You girls may be the victims of a mass hallucination, but I do believe you believe that you saw demons, so I will help in whatever way I can short of facing the demons myself as I am too old and frail for that, and frankly, I am not sure you have seen them except in your minds. First, it would be advisable to know what demons you are facing. Real or unreal, knowledge is a precursor to tackling any problem."

He motioned the girls over to a large alcove in the corner of his office. He walked over to a bookcase filled with volumes of dust covered books, pulled down three large voluminous books and placed them on a long table. He pointed at three chairs by the table and said, "There you are. Look at these illustrations. Every known demon is in these books. First and foremost we need to know the demons you think you are facing and there are ancient and solemn Jewish incantations that are said to have the power to keep these demons at bay, ban them from a place for all time."

LYNTON BUYS A NEW CELL-PHONE

For what seemed like hours, the girls poured over the books. Yet, they did not recognize anything close to what they had seen rise from the stream and rush toward the house. Just as they were about to give up, Ingrid shouted, "Here, here is that abominable creature."

The professor, who had retired to his desk and was grading papers, rushed to the alcove as Lynton and Channa leaped up and stood behind Ingrid, staring at that which was indeed the demon they had seen.

The professor shook his head emphatically, his white hair flailing about. "No, no, it cannot be. It cannot be."

Lynton very calmly said, "It is professor. It is that which we saw. There is no doubt about it."

The professor, shaking his head, was insistent. "I tell you it cannot be. It cannot."

Lynton, looking down at the picture said, "That is the demon, only he is much more ferocious looking when he is standing."

The professor looked down at the illustration again. He began to babble something incomprehensible, shaking his head right to left. Then he muttered, "Can't be. Impossible. Absolutely impossible."

LYNTON BUYS A NEW CELL-PHONE

Channa, in her precise, proper and decisive manner said, "That is the entity. I and my friends know what we saw. There is no room for error with me or with them. My mind is as sharp as a tack when it comes to preciseness. I see something and I record it mentally, file it away with extreme accuracy and recall it in detail."

The professor bent over Ingrid, placed his hand on the page, turned it and there they were, the other two demons in silhouette that they saw.

Lynton, with a bit of frustration in her voice, said, "The other two. The other two. That is them."

The professor sighed and said, "It just can't be. It can't."

The girls looked down at the caption under the picture – *Baal and Nimrod – these two always accompany the devil's right hand man, Belmoda.* Then Lynton turned the page back to the other demon and the girls read its caption, which sent cold chills up and down their spines: *Belmoda, the worst of all demons and the devil's most trusted compatriot. Wherever he appears, the gates to hell are nearby, because he never strays far from those gates so that he can escape back into the bowels of evil where he dwells.*

The professor, shaking his head adamantly, said "This is bad, very bad. The gates to hell are near that house. Yes, the gates to hell."

LYNTON BUYS A NEW CELL-PHONE

Lynton, with unwavering determination, said, "So, you are saying that those demons rising up from that stream bed are coming directly from hell and that the entrance to hell is right there in those people's back yard?"

"I am," said a bewildered professor who sighed and paced up and down in front of a bookcase rubbing his forehead as he continued. "Defeating Belmoda and his henchmen cannot be accomplished. They are demons of the first order that cannot be exorcised. Only they, themselves can decide whether they leave or not. Their power is almost absolute, absolute except for love."

The professor pointed to his desk and the motioned for the girls to follow him. He pointed to the sofa where the three girls took a seat. He sat for a few seconds as in deep thought. He rubbed his chin and contemplated. Then, he looked directly at Lynton and said, "So, you are brave and willing to do battle?"

"I am, and so are my friends," replied a determined Lynton.

Ingrid nodded affirmatively and Channa, of course, used her now pat phrase. "Ready and willing to kick demon butt!"

"OK girls. First, I must share some stories with you. I do not ask you to believe them. Hey, I am not even sure I believe them. Nonetheless, they are necessary for you to understand the daunting task before you. Necessary for you to understand that going into battle against demons is not to be taken lightly. There are forces that none of us understand. I am not a religious man myself, although I am in the Department of Theology. However, I am a reasonably intelligent person who knows there are things that simply cannot be explained; things that are beyond the ability of the human mind to comprehend. Call it another dimension, call it heaven or hell. The point is that some things are unexplainable."

LYNTON BUYS A NEW CELL-PHONE

Lynton leaned forward and said, "We know that professor. We saw things that we cannot believe, but we know we saw them. We heard the cries of lost souls, too. We could not see them either, but we know they were there. We are healthily sceptical about things. We do not accept the words of pontificators of intolerance any more than we accept that which cannot be proved. However, we know what we saw. Call it another dimension, call it heaven, hell or anything else and it does not matter. All we care about is helping two people who have been the vanguard against evil for almost twenty years, and those poor lost souls who await the release from their torment. Maybe they will fade from existence, maybe they will go to heaven if it exists, but their souls are in purgatory now and crying for relief from their misery. We are good and kind women with compassionate hearts. All we want to do is help. A voice on a phone has guided and directed us. Now, we look to you for guidance. Please tell us if there is anything we can do?"

"I do not know, Lynton. I am an old man who has learned that the more I know, the more I need to know. Let me share a bit of knowledge with you as I proposed before."

He leaned back and began a discourse that would raise more questions than it answered. "First, life is warfare. We wage a constant battle against things that are often beyond our control. In an economic system based on greed, we are all on a precipice where one mistake, one illness, the loss of a job can hurl us into an abyss of despair where no one will give us a hand up. Those in poverty, rather than being lifted up, are scorned by a society that thinks poverty is the fault of those who live in it. This world is cruel, unforgiving and harsh beyond any form of decency. Is it any wonder that people turn to religion in hopes of finding in an afterlife that which they were denied in this life. The church is the refuge of the poor. The poor need religion, because they have no other hope."

"Now, is there a heaven or hell? Will it indeed be as difficult for a rich man to get to that so-called heaven as it will for a camel to get through the eye of a needle? Those are unanswerable questions that have plagued mankind and will forever plague him. Are there really demons? Did a man called Jesus perform miracles and cast out demons? There is no definitive answer for me, but I do know that evil exists as sure as I am sitting here conversing with three beautiful women. I see your beauty. I see the inner beauty you all three possess. That is real."

"Although I have not seen demons, I know they exist, because I see the demons of greed, pride, lying, murder of innocents, deceit and discord every day. Evil corrupts and destroys. The evil of greed is avaricious and devours human beings in the eternal march for profits at any cost. People never have enough. The man with a hundred million pesos wants two hundred million. The one with one billion wants two billion."

LYNTON BUYS A NEW CELL-PHONE

Lynton, looking out the window at the sun moving down the sky in the west, was worried that time was running out for them. The professor could see her concern and smiled as he said, "Do not worry pretty one. I am getting to the point."

He leaned back in his chair and continued. "So, is there a Satan? Yes, there is a Satan. He exists in all of us to some degree or another, just as justness, which represents God, also lies within us. The goodness in us must be on guard at all times, because Satan is our adversary. This devil is roaring lion and walks about within us and others, seeking to devour our souls."

"There are forces of light and there are forces of darkness. They are in a constant battle, and the darkness wins more than it loses. Deceit and lies bring us down. These demons from the pits of hell are usually unseen. They only manifest themselves in the open on occasions when they cannot bore within the souls of those they seek."

LYNTON BUYS A NEW CELL-PHONE

The professor again looked directly at Lynton. "My dear, you have a radiant glow about you. I see in you goodness, as I also see it in your two friends, but there is something special about your glow. You give off that special light of a woman who is filled with compassion, but you also have an inner glow that comes, not just from you, but from another source. You child are in love. I say to you that there is only one thing that can defeat Belmoda – one thing. Look within yourself, and you will find the courage to face this demon. I cannot guarantee you victory, but I can tell you that your love can defeat this evil. You must figure out how to reason with a demon who knows no reason to exist but to do evil."

Lynton got up and smiled at the old man. She looked at Ingrid and Channa. She said with a determined countenance, "Girls, let's go. The professor has supplied me with what I need to know. I am ready to go into battle, and I have my two mighty warriors by my side."

The professor smiled proudly, because he knew that Lynton understood what he was saying. Ingrid and Channa were bewildered and confused, but they were loyal and devoted. Understand or not, they would be by Lynton's side.

The three girls walked out of the office, down the hallway and out into the bright light of hope. Terror waited for them behind that old house, but they were ready to walk into the lion's den, and not fear the beast.

CHAPTER 7
FREED THEM FROM THEIR AGONY

Never is hatred stilled by hatred;
it will only be stilled by non-hatred.
This is an eternal law.
Let a person remove anger,
And root out all pride.
No sufferings overtake a person
who neither clings to mind-and-body
nor claims anything of the world.
Conquer anger by non-anger.

LYNTON BUYS A NEW CELL-PHONE

Conquer evil by good.
Conquer miserliness by liberality.
Conquer a liar by truthfulness.
Good and kindness destroy evil.

On the way back to the house, Ingrid and Channa looked puzzled, seemingly waiting for Lynton to explain how she was going to defeat Belmoda. She looked at them, let out a slight giggle and said, "I know what you want. I shall give it to you in a parable."

With supreme confidence and resolve she began a parable. "I shall relate a tale of a demon with a peculiar diet. It seems he fed on the anger of others. And as his feeding ground was the human world, there was no lack of food for him. He found it quite easy to provoke a family quarrel, or national and racial hatred. Even to stir up a war was not very difficult for him. And whenever he succeeded in causing a war, he could properly gorge himself without much further effort;

because once a war starts, hate multiplies by its own momentum and affects even normally kind and caring people. So the demon's food supply became so rich that he sometimes had to restrain himself from over-eating, being content with nibbling just a small piece of resentment found close-by."

"But as it often happens with successful people, he became rather overbearing and one day when feeling bored he thought: *Shouldn't I try it with God? Angels would be so tasty.* So by magic power he transferred himself to that heavenly realm and was lucky enough to come at a time before God's great judgment seat. There was none in the large heavenly hall and without much ado the demon seated himself on God's empty throne, waiting quietly for things to happen. Soon some angels came to the hall and first they could hardly believe their own divine eyes when they saw that ugly demon sitting on God's throne, squatting and grinning. Having recovered from their shock, they started to shout and lament: *Oh you ugly demon, how can you dare to sit on the throne of our Lord? What utter cheekiness! What a crime! You should be thrown headlong back into hell and straight into a boiling cauldron!*"

"But while the angels were growing angrier, the demon was quite pleased because from moment to moment he grew in size, in strength and in power. The anger he absorbed into his system started to ooze from his body as a smoky red-glowing mist. This evil aura kept the angels at a distance and their radiance was dimmed."

"Suddenly a bright glow appeared at the other end of the hall and it grew into a dazzling light from which God, himself, emerged, the King of Heaven. The bellowing smoke created by the angels' anger parted when he slowly and politely approached the usurper of his throne. He bowed his head to him and said, *'Welcome, friend! Please remain seated. I can take another chair.*

May I offer you the drink of hospitality?' As God spoke friendly words, the demon rapidly shrank to a diminutive size and finally disappeared, trailing behind a whiff of malodorous smoke which likewise soon dissolved."

Channa, still perplexed, said, "Damn Lynton!"

Ingrid chortled, "Lynton, I am more confused than ever. You sound like Wayne more every day. You are now using storytelling to make a point. The only trouble is that I am not sure what the point is."

Lynton laughed and as they were getting out of Channa's car, the three girls looked over at the house and saw the shadows of the sun disappearing gradually behind the roof. Time was short."

Demons are classified as supernatural beings that have the power to harm people. Tradition has several terms to discuss demons of different sorts, and there are more stories about demons and demonic bedevilment than there seem to be about ghosts. Often times, the definitions for these terms will change from one source to another, causing overlap and confusion which sometimes even include discussions about ghosts. The term Mazzikin, for example, is used in some cases to talk about destructive spirits of the dead, but can also refer to destructive spirits created on the eve of the last day of creation in the biblical story of Genesis. The concept of destructive creatures created at the very end of the Six Days of Creation also finds expression in creatures known as Shedim, which are also alternately called Lillin when they are described as being the descendants of the mythological figure Lilith. These demons are described as "serpent-like" and are sometimes depicted as human forms with wings, as well. The stories often include descriptions of children being killed in their cradles or some kind of sexualized element, much like traditional succubi.

LYNTON BUYS A NEW CELL-PHONE

This is what the girls had also learned from the professor and they knew that what was waiting for them across the street defied the categories previously mentioned. The three demons there were the most powerful of all demons. These girls had little in the way of concrete religious beliefs, so they feared they might not be mightily armed enough to ward off that which they were about to face.

Ingrid quickly said, "I must go in my house and see my mother. I want to tell her I love her." There was a note of finality in her voice, but no fear, and then she continued as she walked way, "I will be right back. Don't go without me. We three will do this together."

Channa and Lynton stood by her car, gazing over at the house, they discussed how none of the information previously reviewed was relevant to the demons that inhabited the ground around a house where apparently an entrance to hell was opening up to let three of the foulest, most despicable demons loose in search of the souls they craved.

Channa called her boyfriend almost out of instinct. For some reason, Lynton did not call Wayne, because she knew how he worried about her. If she told him what she was about to do, he would hop on the next plane to stand by her side and protect her. She was young, filled with bounding energy, brimming with vitality, permeating with vigour and in all likelihood in much better physical condition than Wayne. Still his masculine instincts made him believe it was his duty to protect her from harm. That was why she loved him so much. It was the reason she had turned her heart and soul over to him. He was the first man in her life who loved her unconditionally. He looked at her and saw no flaws, only perfection. In his eyes she was the embodiment of exquisite purity and virtue. She was the sunshine that lit up his life.

She became teary-eyed as she thought of his warmth, his soft touch; his strong arms that pulled her to him and made her feel so safe. She reflected on their parting at the airport and how she fought back tears to keep him from seeing the depth of her sorrow at his leaving. Reflecting on that day, as Channa chortled away to her boyfriend as if she was in no danger, she intuitively mused on Wayne's parting words: "Never has it been for me that love knows not its own depth until the hour of separation. I love you Lynton Viñas."

Ingrid came back from her house, reflecting on how her mother looked at her as if she were crazy, because never before had she just walked up to her, without any reason, put her arms around the aging woman and blurted out, "I love you mother."

Channa, with an "I love you," quickly hung up the phone and looked at the other two girls.

LYNTON BUYS A NEW CELL-PHONE

The depth and strength of human character are defined by its moral reserves. People reveal themselves completely only when they are thrown out of the customary conditions of their life, for only then do they have to fall back on their reserves. These girls had such love for one another that their true strength came from the bond that chained them like forged steel to each other. They all knew that a caterpillar was a precursor to the butterfly. All their lives they had been caterpillars of contemplation more than action. But today they were butterflies of hope. They were in full bloom. Chests puffed out, shoulders back and determination edged on their beautiful, soft, glowing faces; this was the moment in their hearts when that extraordinary thing called love and confidence in one another melded them into one a shining beacon of hope. They were unafraid, because they knew it was not length of life that counted, but depth of life. They knew that fear of the darkness could make you descend into despair,   but they also knew that the exact measure of your worth was that within you which fortified you to aspire to reach unimaginable heights as you faced adversity with unyielding determination.

Channa looked at Ingrid and Lynton. A little smile pursed her lips. Ingrid gazed at Channa and Lynton, her eyes sparking with resolve. Lynton, a wide grin slowly creeping across her lips looked at the two girls almost laughing. She was like Wyatt Earp ready to lead his deputies to the O.K. Corral. The words were sparse, but they spoke volumes about this demure, diminutive woman with the courage of a lion. "Let's go!"

Channa stood defiant like a bronze statue glistening in the noonday sun and uttered determinedly, "Why not?"

Ingrid bit her lower lip, gave out a half laugh as she looked at Channa, "Yeah, let's go across the street and kick some demon butt!"

LYNTON BUYS A NEW CELL-PHONE

All three laughed for an instance, but quickly the laughter was muted as a look of valorous steadfast tenacity descended upon them. They boldly began to stroll slowly across the street like sheriffs ready to face gunslingers in a western movie. They moved forward, as if nothing could keep them from their appointed task. There eyes were focused on the house, and the duty they felt to those two people who lived there and to those souls that longed to be freed from their agony.

CHAPTER 8
BELMODA WEPT

The daughters of hope
Cannot be consumed by flames.
They march against demons.
Purity pumps from their hearts
In veins of molten rock
To tear demons apart.
Storms of their purity prevail.
These girls vow not to fail.
Be careful their ire not to rile.

LYNTON BUYS A NEW CELL-PHONE

Lava pours like the falling rains
Quakes of determination spew forth,
Shaking them free of demon chains.

They ride forth on horses of hope,
Steeds born of angelic untainted-ness.
They await the call to gather arms
For war that tethers against fate.
Swords held high with righteous fury
These women fight for love's sake.
The darkness of hell blights
out the brightness of day
With evil gloomy shadows spreading
From demons seeking souls.
These princesses of light
Are bold and ready to fight.
Do not mistake their womanliness
With a lack of verve and determinedness.
They fear no demons of the night,
For they carry the righteous light.
So cower you demons of the dark.
These three can destroy you with one spark.

J. WAYNE FRYE

LYNTON BUYS A NEW CELL-PHONE

Lynton, the only one with firm knowledge of what must be done, had four compatriots who did not question her reasoning. They all put their trust in her. She ordered Richard to get picks and shovels quickly before nightfall.

All five of them then proceeded out to the stream in the backyard. Looking carefully along the bank, Lynton said, "We must find the gate to the land where darkness rules. Rather than fight these demons on a battlefield of their choosing, we will fight them in their own lair. I am armed with a weapon that will keep Belmoda at bay and along with him, the evil of his henchmen, Baal and Nimrod, so the souls within that house, along with Richard and Celeste, will be rid of this evil for good, because I am about to go into hell and when I come back I shall close the gates behind me, forcing these demons to find another opening where they can manifest their evil. I cannot end the evil, because as long as there is avaricious greed, envy and gluttony of purpose among men I can only slay it in this place right now and ban it from here, because we five are free of those deadly sins which manifest this evil."

As they all scurried along the creek bank looking for some sign of an opening to the nether world, Lynton continued. "Celeste and Richard have kept these demons at bay, protecting those souls within that house which so many think is an abomination, but that house is in reality a sanctuary, a refuge against evil demons. Those souls will be free tonight or I will be joining them. I am armed with the weapon that may defeat the evil, but I am not certain. That is why when we find the opening, I must go in alone."

Ingrid and Channa adamantly protested, but Lynton explained that with three of them they would be more vulnerable, because the demons were capable of great deceptions. If one of them fell for the deception, the others would be put in jeopardy. This way, going one at a time there was greater chance of success. She pointed back to the house and said, "In my purse is the ancient five page parchment of Jewish rights to fight these three demons that I very discretely removed from the professor's alcove. I read it on our way back here from his office. There is only one way to fight these three demons. It is the only method that has ever been known to work. It is the last one listed. If I do not return, read it and follow the instructions implicitly.

As the girls were talking, Richard shouted, "Look!" He was pointing down at an area just slightly above the waterline on the embankment. There was a red discolouration that stood out from the dark earth that surrounded it. Picks and shovels started flaying about as they dug furiously until they uncovered what appeared to be an iron door that opened inward.

Lynton looked back at her compatriots and said, "I shall close it behind me and you four go back to the house. It will be dark soon. You must go to protect yourselves."

Ingrid hugged Lynton tightly, and Channa joined her. Ingrid said, "He may torment you, but he has no power to harm you, because you have love, our love on your side. You do not walk alone. We will be there with you, because you carry our love. His fury is very great on account of the souls that escape him and he wants those souls trapped in that house. We are all that stands between him and the victory of evil over good."

Lynton smiled and said, "Tell Wayne that I love him more than life itself. Tell him that my last thoughts were of him."

Lynton pushed the door inward, walked into a large cavern, turned and closed the door behind her. It made a ghastly hollow echoing noise, as if she were shutting the door on her tomb.

LYNTON BUYS A NEW CELL-PHONE

Lynton moved forward through the dark caverns, and the only light was bright red glowing rocks along the side walls. She could hear faint moaning in the distance. It was the moans of the lost, the hopeless, those whose souls had been captured and forever trapped in the bowels of a private hell that was locked in another dimension where few, save brave people like her, dared venture. She knew the dimension would be open to her, because those who had seen the demons had the gift of dimensional sight that afforded them perceptive insights not available to most mortals.

Lynton felt like she was in Dante's inferno. She reflected on those souls caught in that house who had temporarily escaped damnation and made it to the Purgatory of that home, a place where the dew of repentance washed off the stain of sin and girded the spirit with humility. Through contrition, confession, and satisfaction by works of righteousness, they had avoided this place of damnation, but the demons wanted them, wanted to trap them in this evil place for eternity.

She began what was to be a kaleidoscopic journey of light, sound and horror. She was working her way ever forward as she continued through the various stages of torment suffered by those trapped there. Poor souls writhed in pain, agony and misery, but none seemed to notice her. It was as if she was invisible, but the suffering she saw was completely visible to her. She began to weep for those trapped there. The smell of sulphur penetrated her nostrils and surged down her throat into the pit of her stomach causing nausea. She felt the need to regurgitate but held it back.

She suddenly found herself amidst a rain of hot and steamy water that seared the flesh. There were naked bodies twitching in agony, lying in a filthy mixture of shadows, brimstone and putrid water. There was a horrid, monstrous size three-headed doglike creature that went from body to body clawing at them, causing agonizing pain. Its growls and hisses sounded like squeals of happiness in the pain it was causing. There was merriment to its solitude enjoyment of making these people pay for transgressions.

She came to a river that had a metal footbridge across it which scorched her feet as she made her way over it. However, there was not water in the river. It was a river of molten fire. It was filled with bodies burning but not disintegrating from the heat. They were stretching out hands seemingly pleading for mercy where there was none. As she got across the river of fire, she came onto more bodies gurgling and shaking in the black mud, slothful and sullen, withdrawn and screaming with agony. Their lamentations bubbled to the surface as they all seemed to be repeating a doleful plea for forgiveness of the sins of gluttony and avaricious greed. Obviously these were people who had lived a cruel life devoid of compassion and love for their fellow man. Each step forward made Lynton weary and forlorn. She knew the punishment was just reward for a life lived with no compassion for those who suffered from poverty, neglect and loneliness. Yet, she, being the kind hearted woman she was, could not help but pity these people who had made their own personal hell through a life of excess.

She approached what appeared to be a wretched city where she beheld a wide plain surrounded by red hot iron walls. Before her lay fields of writhing bodies shaking from discontent, distress and terrible torment. Burning bodies that were not consumed by the flames littered the landscape. Then she moved past a giant circle where infernal furies stained with blood and the torn limbs of those poor souls who were trapped there minus parts of their bodies.

A hairy creature that was half man, half bear snarling in fury, snapped at her as she moved steadily forward. Its teeth were grinding together as anticipating the biting of her flesh. Yet, she flinched not and showed no fear. She moved by a lake filled with boiling blood that had the stench of death and decay as body parts bobbed on the surface. Head bowed and sweat pouring off her brow she trudged ever forward toward he whom she sought. Finally passing the lake, she stepped onto scorching sand where moaning men and women were being bombarded with flakes of fire raining down against their naked bodies.

She came upon a giant pit of despair where people were struggling, clawing and pleading to be let out as molten droplets of fire thrown by horned demons rained down on them. The demons looked at Lynton and licked their lips as if anticipating getting her in the pit soon. She wanted to close her eyes from the terror of the pain she witnessed and then put them over her ears to drown out the cries of agony. Yes, she knew these people had lived horrible lives filled with gluttony and disregard for fairness that justified punishment and damnation, but her kind heart simply could not fathom making people suffer as she was witnessing. Surely there should be an end to this? Surely eternity was too long to pay for the sins of wrath, greed, slothiness, pride, lust, envy and gluttony.

She arrived at a vast open plain of red sand and in the distance was a golden throne that had fire rising from it. She edged closer and a hideous creature sitting on the throne came into view. It was Belmoda and standing on each side of him was Nimrod and Baal.

Belmoda's mouth was gushing bloody foam and his eyes were fiery beacons that pierced through to your soul with a promise of damnation. There was no light here, and despite what should have been tremendous heat from the surrounding fires and the hot, barren sand, there was an intense coldness that made Lynton shiver.

LYNTON BUYS A NEW CELL-PHONE

Belmoda greeted her with a nod. She feared him not, because this was why she made the journey. She was willing to face the horrors of this demon's lair to save those people above. How do your fight the devil's right hand man – the archangel of despair? Was there any power short of God, who Lynton had doubts existed, that can match wits with this evil minion of despair?

Belmoda's horns glistened against the intense fires burning behind him. Looking Belmoda directly in his eyes, Lynton asked herself who was God? And like a light bulb bringing instant light to a darkened room at the flip of a switch, she suddenly realized that Belmoda, who stood at least ten feet tall and was as wide as a basketball court and breathed smoke from his nostrils did not have to be defeated physically. She had read the ancient Jewish parchment, but until this very moment she had not realized the meaning at the end, where it simply said, *LOOK WITHIN.*

Lynton realized she had God within her. In her own way she was God, because of the goodness in her. Each individual had God within, but they also had the devil, and there was a constant battle between the two. For far too many people God could not surface, because people through the years, as they grew and matured, fell victim to the culture of greed which used the devil in each person to teach selfishness, self-aggrandizement, gluttony, inhumanity and disregard for kindness and compassion.

Lynton knew she needed no other weapon than love to defeat the demon Belmoda. She looked in his fiery eyes that were blueprints for evil of the foulest kind and she projected love. Yes, she pitied him for having to serve the devil. She felt sorry for this demon that had to bow before evil. Love had nurtured Lynton. You could see it in her eyes, in her countenance, in her soul. Belmoda had never known such love, because he had served the prince of evil.

Belmoda's eyes began to reflect the love Lynton had shared for so many years with her father, her mother, her siblings, her aunt and uncle, and, of course, now with Wayne. She was respected and admired by all who knew her. She was a woman who knew no anger. She knew no hatred, no greed. Compassion ruled her soul.

Lynton was a woman who knew that love comes to those who give it, not to those who seek it. It was a binding force that lifted the spirits of the weak and weary. Love sought harmonious contentment for those who ached. It was the spark that lit the flame of purpose in men's hearts. It was the builder of hope with heaven's delight in the midst of hell's despair.

Belmoda bowed his head and pointed back toward the way Lynton had come. He flared his nostrils and belched smoke, which made Lynton assume she had just lost her battle with the mighty Belmoda.

Even as deep, as pure, as intense as was Lynton's love, a demon of evil, second only to the devil himself, could not be swayed. He would not succumb to that which he had no concept of in his barren heart.

Lynton had long ago forgotten the Bible verses that were forced upon her to make her obedient to those who wanted to control her thoughts and emotions. All she could remember was the shortest verse in the Bible: "Jesus wept."

She looked at Belmoda – Belmoda the terrible. The demon suddenly sucked in air and grew larger and larger. In his eyes, Lynton saw doubt. Belmoda stood and again pointed toward the way from which Lynton had come.

She raised her head and knew she had won. Belmoda pointed again to the way she had come. Belmoda had tears in his eyes. The evil minion of despair wept.

EPILOGUE

HELLO

There was euphoria in the house, and as Lynton walked in there was a feeling of peace all about. Channa, Ingrid, Celeste and Richard all embraced her fondly and Channa offered good news. "Lynton, it must have been at the very moment you defeated Belmoda. There was a peace that came over the house and sweet smells of lilac were all about. The poor souls trapped here have been released. I know they have."

LYNTON BUYS A NEW CELL-PHONE

Peace and harmony had returned to the old house on Garibaldi Road. Richard and Celeste no longer had to fear the night. The evil had been conquered by three women who refused to bow before the ill winds of despair.

Wayne had once told Lynton, "For me there lies within the lights and shadows of your eyes, the beauty of your soul. I see not the exterior. I see the inside that glistens with goodness. That is the woman I love. That is the woman I glorify in the far reaches of my mind. That is what shines like a beacon when I am in darkness and despair. That is the base upon which my love stands gloriously unbowed, unashamed in the bright sunshine of hope."

What Wayne had told Lynton seemed to reverberate in her mind. Love was at the centre of what defeated Belmoda, and love was at the very core of the relationship between Lynton, Ingrid and Channa. And, of course, the love of Wayne was what fortified Lynton when she faced the terror perpetrated by Belmoda, Nimrod and Baal.

Real love is a scarce commodity in today's world where instant romance on the internet is as readily available as instant coffee to give a person that morning jolt of caffeine, instant microwave food to titillate the taste buds or even the instant absolution of sin if enough money is put in the collection plate. Everything in the modern world of corporate capitalism comes with a price tag, but Wayne and Lynton had decided there was no price tag on love.

Lynton gripped the cell-phone. No, she caressed it as if it was her life-link to Wayne. She longed for him, longed to be in his arms and feel secure. With him, she knew she had a champion to defend her and protect her from harm.

Suddenly, Lynton's cell phone rang, and all there with her assumed it was that voice again, but Lynton looked at the number display and realized it was Wayne. She shook her head and said, as it continued to ring, "Oh, no. It is Wayne. I haven't called him for three days. You think Belmoda was tough to deal with. That was a piece of cake compared to dealing with my Wayne. Hello…………………..................................

THE END

**Don't miss these exciting
Young Readers Series Books by J. Wayne Frye**

Lynton Curls Her Hair

**Hockey Mania and the Mystery
of Nancy Running Elk**

**White Meteors and the Ghost
of Sue Ann McGee**

**How Hockey Saved a Jew
From the Holocaust: The Rudi Ball Story**

**Available from your local bookstore
Or
Amazon.com**

The Real Lynton Viñas

VOCABULARY
(Taken from the Oxford Canadian Dictionary)

Prologue:

clandestine – done secretly

mystique – an air of mystery

demeanour – a person's appearance or behaviour

wiles – a way of ensnaring or deceiving to get what you want

Chapter 1

magnanimous – having or showing a generous and kind nature

anticipatory – to anticipate something

vamping – a woman using charm to seduce and control men

titillate – to interest or excite

libido – sexual drive

Giddy – playful, silly, showing great joy

naught – nothing

acquiesced – accept, agree, allow

lamenting – to express sorrow, regret, or unhappiness

pensiveness – dreamingly thoughtful

Chapter 2

revelry – merrymaking

intonate – to suggest in clear tones

savoir-faire – to behave in a proper, confident way

euphoria – a feeling of well-being or elation

propaganda – false or exaggerated statements to help a cause

bauble – inexpensive piece of jewellery

inherently – the basic nature of someone

simultaneously – at eh same time

hone – make more acute, more effective or intense

glib – said or done carelessly

rendition – a performance of something

inflection – change in pitch or loudness

insidious – causing harm

levity – lack of seriousness - amusing

aggrandizes – to make great or greater

Chapter 3

damsels – a young woman

sari-sari store – Philippine term for small neighbourhood convenience store, usually part of a house

acrimonious – angry and bitter

camaraderie – friendship among a group

tarry – slow in going

pall – smoothing covering a place

lecher – man with a disgusting interest in sex or a woman

demeanour – person's appearance or behaviour

ambiance – mood or feeling of a place

unmitigated – not lessened or changed

gingerly – cautious or very careful

permeate – to pass through or all around

discombobulated – upset or confused

consternation - worry

scrutiny – closely observe

mumbo-jumbo – superstitious

vile – evil, immoral, unpleasant

diabolical – very evil

amiss – something wrong

transfixed – fixed upon, highly concentrated on something

manifestations – an occurrence, a happening

prophetic – stating the future correctly

melodic – pleasing or agreeable tot eh ear

comeliness – pleasing appearance

arduous – difficult, not easy

clarion – clear and precise

Chapter 4

writhing – twist or distort

transfixed – concentrated on something

elongated – very long

malevolent – evil

Wolf-bane – plant thought to ward-off werewolves

fanciful – coming from the imagination, unusual

emanating – to come out from a source

cavalcade – a procession or line of things

cower – to shake or move back in fear

cataclysmic – violent or momentous event or upheaval

nook – small space or corner

cranny – obscure nook or corner

unabated – not stopping
abominations – horribly evil
trepidation – fear
staid – serious, boring, old-fashioned
penance – something given or an act to show you are sorry
self-aggrandizement – praising ones self
platitudes – compliments
purgatory – place where souls are made pure by suffering
inherent – basic nature of something
nigh – close in time or place, nearly
recompense – payment for loss or suffering
excruciating – very painful
insidious – very harmful
Chapter 5
vanguards – those at the forefront, the first to guard
pined – to long for something or somebody
germane – relevant and appropriate
subterfuge – deception or tricks to get something
cadence – regular beat or rhythm to something
gait – the stride or way a person walks
abject – utterly hopeless
penchant – strongly inclined
abominable – awful, horrible
conduit – a natural passage
immoderately – extreme, exceeding the reasonable
Chapter 6
incarnate – embodied in the flesh, exactness
cognizant – aware of
sage – valuable, dependable, wise
acquiesced – to give into
vamped – to entice or lure usually by seductive means
precursor – precedes
emphatically – with great emphasis
compatriot – someone who is of similar background
adamantly – unyielding
exorcised – to expel or free a person of evil spirits
pontificators – to speak in a arrogant, all-knowing manner
precipice – thee dge of a cliff
avaricious – greedy, coveting

countenance – appearance, especially look on the face
Chapter 7
malodorous – unpleasant or offensive odour
cheekiness – impudent, without politeness
Mazzikim – a harmful spirit made on the 6th day of creation
Shedim – Hebrew word for demon
Lillin – Hebrew spirit
Lilith – Hebrew demon
Succubi – a demon in female form
permeating – pass through, every part of
chortled – gleefully expressed
intuitively – knowing something
precursor – before, preceding
inexactitude – not accurate
melded – to blend
steadfast – firm, resolute
tenacity – determined, unyielding
Chapter 8
lair – a den or resting place, a hideout
parchment – an old manuscript or document (old paper)
implicitly – expressly stated without reservations
embankment – a part out of the water
regurgitate – to give back or repeat/to throw-up
lamentations – expressing grief
gluttony – excessive eating or drinking/too much
avaricious – greedy/wanting it all
doleful – mournful
forlorn – very sad
Epilogue
reverberate – rebound, recoil, reflected